THE LOST TUNNEL OF SAMOS

THE LOST TUNNEL OF SAMOS

Jane Hartley Schofield

Matador
9 Priory Business Park,
Wistow Road, Kibworth Beauchamp,
Leicestershire. LE8 0RX
Tel: 0116 279 2299
Email: books@troubador.co.uk
Web: www.troubador.co.uk/matador
Twitter: @matadorbooks

ISBN 978 1838594 480

British Library Cataloguing in Publication Data.
A catalogue record for this book is available from the British Library.

Printed and bound in Great Britain by 4edge Limited
Typeset in 11pt Minion Pro by Troubador Publishing Ltd, Leicester, UK

Matador is an imprint of Troubador Publishing Ltd

*To Chris Parker, Tunnelling Engineer,
whose endless enthusiasm and positive determination
to 'get our ducks in a row' inspired us all.
We miss you.*

CONTENTS

"I have dwelt longer upon the history of the Samians than I should otherwise have done, because they are responsible for three of the greatest building and engineering feats in the Greek world: the first is a tunnel nearly a mile long, eight feet wide and eight feet high, driven clean through the base of a hill nine hundred feet in height...along which water from a copious spring is led through pipes into the town.

This was the work of a man named Eupalinos, son of Naustrophos of Megara".

Herodotus, writing about the mid-5th century BC

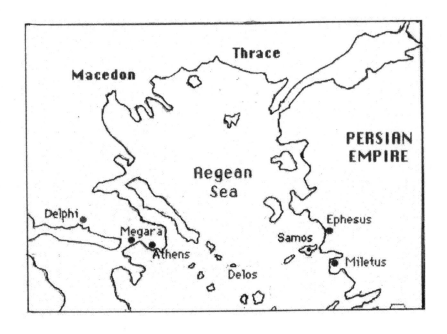

I

The Island of Samos

Look at the Island, hazy in the far distance; a great slab of grey-green rock surrounded by wind and crashing waves. Approaching, you can see that it is fertile in parts and, in other parts nearer the sea, brown and naked.

Come now, and listen, for this is Samos two and a half thousand years ago. Let me tell you the tale of Eupalinos of Megara, a genius, and of Polycrates, the cruel and corrupt tyrant, who summoned him to Samos to complete what must surely be an impossible task.

It is the story of an extraordinary man who, all those centuries ago, managed to construct a marvel, digging blind, relying on nothing but abstract calculations and his own extraordinary understanding of the rules of geometry. What was this marvel? You may well ask.

Herodotus the historian tells us of the three wondrous feats of engineering constructed on Samos at this time, but the greatest marvel of them all, he says, is the extraordinary tunnel which is the subject of this story.

*

Samos, 535 BC
A coup d'etat

Another dry summer, and there is never quite enough water. The old men are angry, the young men sullen. Something will happen soon, they mutter among themselves, if the landlords do nothing.

These landowners' leaders have ruled the island as a comfortable oligarchy for generations, overseeing the working of their lands with their vines and olives, sheep and goats, and exacting heavy tithes from the peasants who work the fields for them. The habits of generations of rich living has lulled them into believing that they are invulnerable to change. But this summer there has been a drought again; the peasants' families are going hungry, for now the water shortage is becoming acute.

Something will surely happen soon. It must.

*

The town is quiet, the citadel on the hill closed and silent. Cool early-morning light glints suddenly on bright metal, just before sunrise, as the armed killers move in quickly, and chickens cluck in alarm, startled out of sleep.

None of the guardsmen on duty up there see them coming. Running along the ridge above the town towards the citadel, these fifteen young warriors catch the guards by surprise; the outer watchman is knocked sideways by a blow to the head and thrown down the cliff-face. Leaping up the steps of the citadel, the killers cut the throats of the two guards at the doors and push their way in to the main chamber of the palace.

They are after the rich landowners' leaders, the aristocrats of Samos who have gathered in the citadel, imagining they will be safe there. The killers hunt them out, chasing them down the narrow corridors, stabbing and slashing and screaming insults as they go. When they are caught, cowering in small dark rooms, they are cut down like oxen for the offering. Then, at last, it is finished; not one is left alive.

Three of the young men, brothers, the leaders of the warrior group, step back outside, dragging the dead men with them to show to the nervous crowd which has been following at a careful distance. In their crested helmets and glittering breastplates, they swagger on the palace steps, towering over the cringing townsfolk below. There is little more they need to do. The brothers fling the bodies down the steps, look at each other, and grin. They are Pantagnostos, Polycrates and Syloson, the sons of the pirate Aeaces, arrogant and ruthless men, all three. They have seized power and can now rule as tyrants of the island of Samos.

*

II

THE GOVERNOR'S
HOUSE IN CHORA

SAMOS, 1853

As usual in the summers here, although the sun had
only just risen, the day would soon become very hot. I
took my drawing pad and a good, soft pencil, and went out
to sit in the courtyard, under the shade of the olive tree. They
call me Eleni; I am a 'poor relation' of the Governor, and I was
already feeling impatient, for I knew that these were almost
the only moments I would have to myself that day. With luck,
though, I might just have time to capture the pattern of shade
cast by the old tree's leaves, before I was called indoors to help
the old lady get dressed and to listen, trying hard to be patient,
to a litany of inconveniences which had occurred during the
night. It was a tiresome occupation.

I should have been grateful to have been taken care of, I
know. I should always remember that, after losing my parents,
the Governor had asked me to come and live with them, as a
sort of companion to his elderly wife. I did try, always, to be
thankful but, oh dear, the tedium of it! I escaped as often as
I could. I loved to sketch the twisted roots of that old tree;

sometimes I think my drawings were the only activity which kept me sane.

The previous evening, at dinner, there had been talk of the arrival of a visitor, a learned man, apparently, from Paris. I let my mind wander as I sketched, wondering what he would be like. Paris! Surely this would be interesting? Anything to animate the conversation, and provide some relief from the tedium of my duties at the Governor's house.

The call came from the darkened bedroom, querulous as always: "Eleni, where are you?"

*

That same morning, Monsieur Victor Guerin, antiquarian connoisseur and amateur archaeologist, stood at the prow of the sailing boat and carefully fingered his waxed moustache. The boat, beating up against the wind from Patmos, north, north-east to the island of Samos, was making heavy headway and Monsieur Guerin, as always, was impatient to arrive.

Arrangements had been made for him to stay at the Governor's house on Samos while he set about his investigations, a courtesy which he found convenient, as well as suitably flattering. He hoped, too, that a good luncheon would have been prepared for him, as they had set sail well before breakfast and he was hungry for sustenance, for the mind and for the stomach, he told himself with satisfaction. This island of Samos was well-known for its three magnificent ancient monuments, none of them, as yet, properly explored and written up. There was much to be done here.

As the ship headed eastwards, running along the southern coast of the island, the remains of a vast, ruined temple came into view near the beach, and Guerin nodded his head enthusiastically. Not long after this, the helmsman swung the prow to port as they entered the famously huge, ancient harbour full of small fishing vessels, and tied up at the untidy quay-side. An uproar broke out as women ran up, shouting at him to buy something, small boys fought to carry his luggage and he was pushed and cajoled towards a line of waiting carters who also fought for the honour of taking him to his final destination. Monsieur Guerin smiled contentedly and, choosing the cleanest-looking cart, dusted the seat with his handkerchief, and they set off.

*

That evening I sat next to the foreign gentleman, listening with interest as he held court. Monsieur Victor Guerin was an archaeologist, and certainly very learned. He was older than I had thought he would be, and rather plump and short, shorter than I am myself. He talked a great deal, and much too loudly, while twirling his waxed moustache, seeming determined to impress upon the company just how erudite a scholar he was.

I found myself fascinated, though, as he spoke about collecting material for his fourteenth book. Having carefully, and at great length, covered all the ancient cities of the Anatolian coast, he was now working his way through the islands of the Eastern Aegean, noting their cultural features and their ancient monuments. This was a work, he explained to the company, which he happily anticipated would take him the rest of his life.

I glanced over at the Governor and his wife. They appeared to be listening politely, but I could see their eyes were glazed; they had little interest in the island's history. Perhaps Monsieur Guerin sensed their disinterest, as he turned now towards me.

"And you, Mademoiselle?" he asked in his heavy accent. "Are you interested in the antiquities of your beautiful country?" I replied that I was indeed. It was a fact that I had never had the opportunity to explore the rich history and culture of this island as I would have liked to, always on call as I was in my role as companion to the Governor's wife. It was rare in my position to meet new people, and this plump little man, though pompous and self-important, shared my interests but knew so much more than I did. Besides, I found his affectations amusing.

After dinner Monsieur Guerin took me aside to ask if he might lend me some articles he had written. He suggested, with a twirl of his moustache, that perhaps we could then discuss them together,.

"Why, certainly you may, Monsieur, I should be honoured to read them," I replied. "You will find I am a very quick reader."

Oh *yes*, how exciting! An opportunity to explore a topic that has long fascinated me; this could be so interesting! Some intellectual stimulation, at last.

A day that had started empty, threatening to be the same routine as every day for almost as long as I could remember, had suddenly become a great deal brighter.

*

I read and read, late into the night. I found my new friend's articles a little dry, I am afraid, but I simply could not put down the book of Histories he was so good as to lend me. Of course, it was written all in ancient Greek, so different from the Greek we speak today, and which I have never had the opportunity to study, but fortunately Monsieur had also supplied me with a modern translation. I was especially thrilled to read what the author had written about Samos, my own island: he wrote that our ancient monuments were the greatest in all of Greece! How proud that made me feel. I was a little puzzled to read about *three* great monuments, though? Our huge ancient harbour is, of course, a wonderful thing, and Hera's temple, further along the shore, is vast and beautiful indeed, but I knew nothing about a tunnel. I wondered why it had been built, and what could have been so special about it.

And then I read about the tyrant Polycrates who, apparently, had freed the people of Samos from the tyranny of their landlords, only to replace that with a tyrannical rule of his own. I let drop the book on to my lap for a while and leant back, trying to imagine what it all might have been like...

*

It is Polycrates, the middle brother, who has organized it. He knows that Samos is ripe for this coup, for certainly none of the peasants will make difficulties. And the landowners' leaders have not reckoned on Aeaces' sons.

The word has been spread to a dozen friends, other loose young men like themselves. These are neither landowners nor peasants but mostly make a living out of piracy, plundering the cargoes of passing ships, or attacking isolated villages on the surrounding islands. His own father, Aeaces, had grown rich in this way, but Polycrates wants more. Killing the men in the citadel has been easy, but there is a power vacuum to be filled now, and quickly. Polycrates, without consulting his brothers, summons certain others of the land-owning aristocracy to a meeting.

They arrive quietly, as night is falling, and are ushered into the great hall of the citadel, where Polycrates sits surrounded by his guards. These landowners, all rich men, and proud, are summarily informed that the lands and possessions of all the murdered men have been seized, and their families reduced to slavery, and they are warned that the same punishment will be handed out to anyone else foolish enough to object.

"Listen" says Polycrates then, "and do what I say. Let me announce to the townspeople tomorrow that you have accepted me to rule as sole tyrant of Samos from now on. The confiscated lands and goods will be divided amongst all of us here if, as I am sure will be the case, you all agree?"

Of course they agree. It is not lost on the landowners that neither of the other two brothers is present at the meeting, but this is not their problem; so much the better for them if the brothers quarrel amongst themselves, they think. And, indeed, the brothers do quarrel, but it will prove to be of no advantage to the landowners.

Pantagnostos, the elder brother, when he hears of the deal, draws his dagger and rushes at his brother in a fury, but Polycrates has his own bodyguards ready. Pantagnostos is seized and imprisoned in the citadel, where he is summarily executed as a traitor. Syloson, the younger brother, is easier to deal with. Polycrates simply banishes him from the island, condemning him to exile, and from then on rules alone. Most of the old aristocracy are also exiled, or flee of their own accord if they can. Those who remain will prove to be a thorn in the tyrant's side, but this will not be until many years later.

Meanwhile, Polycrates is a popular ruler: news spreads quickly that there is money to be had and reputations to be made in Samos. The tyrant's reign has begun in a chaos of violence and bloodshed, yet it seems that the Gods will allow him unparalleled fortune and success, on a scale never before seen. Samos becomes famous and Polycrates, for a while, the most magnificent of rulers.

*

Our visitor and I were sitting under the shade of the tree in the courtyard of the Governor's house. Sunlight played on yellow blocks of stone as tiny lizards flashed and disappeared into the crevices between them.

Monsieur Guerin's arrival had certainly broken the tedium of life at Chora, given quite a focus to our afternoons. I found him both irritating and entertaining, I must admit. Sometimes I wanted to laugh out loud at the extravagance of his manner, but I knew I must be very careful not to let it show

"So the tyrant Polycrates was nothing more than a brigand, was he not?" I was eager to ask Monsieur Guerin's opinion on this, for I had read in the history book that he was just a pirate, the scourge of all the islands hereabouts, a mere thief.

The gentleman was launched upon our favourite subject of history. Upon his arrival at Chora there had been a great many formalities to be completed before the Governor found that he could give his consent for investigations to begin. Meanwhile, our visitor had found in me a most willing listener.

"Certainly he was a pirate", he replied. "Polycrates was the *thalassocrat* of the day, the only Greek ruler at the time who understood that sea power, if he used it properly, could be equal to the land forces of any great kingdom. He had a hundred ships and there was no other state to touch him."

"And so?"

"Well you see, this was politics, *chère Mademoiselle*, a way of dealing with the competition of others, of controlling trade, and establishing political dominance."

I was quite determined to show that I had read the ancient texts which he had lent me, so I may have sharpened my tone a little. "Politics? Was he not just an arrogant plunderer? He did not care who he stole from, a friend or an enemy, for he argued that a friend was better pleased if you gave him back what you had taken from him, than if you spared him at the first."

"*Exactement!*" cried Victor Guérin, happily waving his hands in the air. "You see what a politician he was! Tomorrow

10

we will visit the harbour, and the great walls of the ancient city, and you will see how this piracy and thieving and, yes, this thuggery and violence were the basis of Samos' prosperity, when Polycrates was tyrant."

"Oh, do continue," I exclaimed, amused beyond words at his extravagant hand waving. Monsieur Guerin beamed at me.

"You see, my dear, though the Persians had reached the edge of Asia Minor, they were soldiers, not sailors. They had not conquered the eastern islands of the Aegean, and so Polycrates owed allegiance to no-one. His squadrons were privateers, fought battles, levied tolls; they captured enemy transports and held men and even whole cities to ransom.

"That is how, with their navy, they came to dominate their neighbours on the islands and the mainland of Asia Minor. He aimed at the creation of a naval empire in the Aegean, with a force of one hundred ships and a thousand archers to impose his will. Oh yes, he was a spectacular pirate!"

I had to smile at his enthusiasm. I was finding these conversations delightful; how interesting it was at last, to be able to converse with such a knowledgeable person.

"On the one hand of course, we have the ancient writers, but so much has been lost, just fragments remain, so tantalising. On the other hand, we have the stones beneath our feet but, there again, so much has disappeared, just broken pieces left. Fragments of words, fragments of stone..."

Guerin paused and stared round the garden. It was clear that some of these very stones, bases of columns and lovely pieces of broken marble had, quite recently, been grubbed up and used to build a wall around the Governor's property.

"What can be done to make people value these things?" he now cried out dramatically, turning towards me. Astonished by this sudden change of mood, I tried very hard to look serious. I was beginning to understand just how earnestly Monsieur

Guérin desired to bring the local people to a greater awareness and appreciation of their extraordinary classical heritage.

So, still trying to suppress my smile, I told him, just as earnestly, that I looked forward with pleasure to discovering all that he could show me. As I turned to go back inside the house he bowed politely and followed me in; he was humming a little tune as he walked upstairs. Without wishing to sound vain, I think that may have been when, while looking for his maps, it first occurred to him that it might be very pleasant to have me for a pupil.

*

We had climbed to the top of Mount Kastro, behind the harbour town of Pythagorion, or Tigani, as it was then called. Wandering through the ruined vineyards and the olive groves and the broken old trees full of ripe figs, we went on up past the monastery of St Spillion. There we paused to rest the donkey, and to greet some of the kindly monks who lived there, who offered us olives and cool water to refresh us. I was proud to be able to show off our learned visitor, as I knew that a number of these monks were interested in ancient things.

They expressed their interest in our search, but Monsieur Guerin was becoming impatient by now, and wished to go on.

We left the donkey in their care, and continued on foot up the hillside. With the raw sun hot above us, we turned to look back down over the harbour, far below us, and the red roofs of the little town, and out to the glittering, white-capped sea.

On we went, still higher, treading now over bare rocks and wild thyme, until we came up at last to the old *castro*. We sat down on a striped blanket under a fig tree looking out over the Strait of Mycale, the narrow strip of sea which separates

Samos from the Turkish mainland. A gentle breeze blew the hair from my face, and bees hummed in the wild thyme.

"Just over there" Guerin reminded me, "were the prosperous cities of Ionia – emigrants from Greece, centuries before. But like their countrymen back in the motherland, they were too quarrelsome to present a united front to the Persians. Cyrus the Great, the Persian king, with his general, Harpagon the Mede, were able to pick them off one by one, and they were brutally subdued. Those who submitted were allowed to live, but cities which tried to hold out were ravaged, their leaders killed and their population enslaved.

"Unspeakable cruelties were meted out to defeated enemies. They might be flayed alive, fed to animals or impaled. So terrible was the cruelty of the barbarians that their coming remained in folk memory for generations."

I was silent, looking at the Turkish coastline over the water, so close it seemed one could almost have swum across. Behind us, the colossal stones of the ancient defences still formed parts of a circular rampart six kilometres long, with the remains of great towers at strategic points. Local people still called this part of the mountain the Acropolis.

Once, it had hummed with bustle and movement, but there was nothing but silence now. No one came up here any more. The stones lay where they had fallen, huge and solid and stationary, baking slowly in the heat. Nothing moved, except for the slight breeze waving the dry, brown grass, and a hawk, circling high above us.

I leaned back on to the warm marble, broken now, and tumbled, and thought of the town it used to enclose, with flat-roofed, white-washed mud brick and stone houses in a maze of busy little streets and alleyways, cobbles and stairways and cisterns, with goats and chickens penned in small yards, and fig trees struggling to grow between the rocky outcrops. People lived up here then. They, too, looked out across the water, and must have trembled as they watched the fires burning on the mainland, as other towns and cities crumbled.

Would their swaggering, pleasure-loving tyrant be able to protect them from the barbarians? Or would it have been safer to treaty, to give in to the Persian and live the humiliation of submission? For all the subjects of the Great King were his slaves.

Monsieur Guérin was striding away across the mountain, talking and waving his hands as he went.

"As you can see, these walls were three metres thick and six metres high, and they continued, as I said, for over six kilometres. *Regardez!* Some of them remain intact, and their construction is admirable. There were also square towers, but most of them are gone now. Some of this, undoubtedly, was built on the remains of much older fortifications, but however that may be, it is my opinion that we have here the most perfect specimen of military architecture in Greek antiquity!"

I wished he would slow down a little, as I hurried after him. "Monsieur, please, I hardly know how to keep up," I called.

"Do you ask me how it was done?" Guerin called back, expectantly. "Ah, it is Herodotus the Historian who tells us: *'The prisoners Polycrates took were forced to dig, in chains, the moat which surrounds the stronghold in the capital city of Samos.'* And who were these unfortunate prisoners? They were Greeks! The people of Miletus, from Lesbos, whom he had defeated at sea."

Monsieur Guérin's voice became fainter as he strode away across the enclosed area, and I found myself laughing again in spite of myself, as I struggled to follow him over the rough stones. He called back over his shoulder to point out how, far below us, the fortifications reached right down to the sea-shore. I should look down at the harbour, he instructed, where the little town of Tigani crouched at our feet, between the mountain and the sea.

Far below we could just hear the faint clack-clack of halyards on the masts of ships, tapping and creaking in the wind. From where we stood, high up, the harbour did indeed seem to be in the shape of a frying pan, which I know is the old meaning of the word *tigani*.

"It is more likely," he corrected me "that the name is a corruption of the word *dogana*, meaning 'customs house', as this was one of the city's functions."

"This is all, now, that is left of that ancient city" he said. "But does it not seem to you to have an unnaturally large harbour? See the breakwater: the mole is two furlongs long and is constructed far out into the deep sea. It protects the port from southerly winds, but it is not natural at all, *non, non, non*. On the contrary, it was also built on the orders of the tyrant, and it is one of the greatest engineering works in the ancient world.

"Why, do you ask? Well, only think of the size of the blocks of stone needed to construct such a thing! They had to be cut, and transported, and placed in position, all in twenty fathoms of water. Pity the poor Miletian prisoners of war; I fear few of them could have survived."

I realised that my teacher was trying to show me more than just the magnificence of ancient stones. Of all the morality tales in the Greek lexicon, this tale of *hubris*, the arrogance of tyrants, has been most clearly spelled out in the history of my poor island of Samos. What has all this magnificence come to? Famous in the ancient world for the scale of the plunder and pillage it wreaked in Polycrates' time, my island has itself been repeatedly ravaged throughout its history since then.

We were still an occupied country, subjected to the rule of the Ottoman Turks, descendants of those very same mainland peoples against whom it seems my people have been battling ever since the time of Troy.

And we were now in the year 1853! The mainland and most of the islands of Greece had at last won their weary, bloody independence from the Ottoman Turks, but the Great Powers of Europe had decreed that Chios, Samos, and a few minor islands should still be ruled by the *Sublime Porte* of Turkey. What is more, all the signs seemed to show that this unfair and unkind state of affairs might continue for years to come.

I remembered how my own family had suffered, and my mood changed: picking up a stone, I hurled it out to sea, towards the Turkish coast.

"Tell me why they are still our enemies," I demanded, "Why has it always been this way?

Victor Guerin gave a little cough. I tried to control my frustration; his reply, I knew, would be an attempt to smooth things over, and I sighed. He had a tendency to change the subject at difficult moments.

"Herodotus begins his Histories with this very question, you know, and that was already a very long time ago. His aim was, in fact, as he writes: *'to show how the two races came into conflict.'*

"He says that it all started with *'nothing worse than woman-stealing'* – those are his very words – when Paris stole Helen from Sparta and took her away to Troy, on what is now the Turkish mainland. But in retaliation the Achaeans invaded Asia and destroyed the Trojans, all on account of a girl from Sparta, and this is why the two peoples have been enemies ever since. Herodotus writes that he has no intention of passing judgement as to whether this version of events is true or false. Remarkable, really..."

Guerin looked at me, and I stared back at him. I was so deeply interested, and I longed to to know more; the better to understand how it was that we island Greeks could have had to suffer so. I determined to encourage him to continue.

"Oh yes, I have so enjoyed reading the Histories which you lent me. It all still sounds so clear and fresh to me. But I am impatient, now", I cried. "I want to learn how to fit together ancient words and ancient stones. What was life really like in those far-off days? What sort of people were they, my ancestors, the ancient Greeks of Samos? Please, I am so anxious to learn!"

Walking back down to where the donkey was tethered, we were silent again. Perhaps Monsieur Guérin was wondering whether he had taken on more than he had realised. I like to think he appreciated my enthusiasm, but I fear he found my forthrightness slightly alarming.

*

III

―――――――――――――――

WE HAVE SO LITTLE information, *ma chère Eleni*, thought Monsieur Guérin, sitting alone in his shady room later that evening. You do not know how difficult. However, I think it may perhaps have been something like this...

... *about 539 BC*

People jostle and push their way through narrow streets in this crowded city. It is mid summer and the heat is intense. Crowds of newcomers fill the city, attracted to Samos by its new-found prosperity: there is money to be made here. Poets and entertainers, artists and artisans, soothsayers, prostitutes, money-lenders and wheelers and dealers of all kinds, all hoping for a chance to share in the wealth generated from the tyrant's extravagant court and his grandiose building plans.

The city is one vast building site. Many of the newly rich are building smart houses, new roads need to be constructed and shops are going up, especially along the Sacred Way leading to the *Heraion*, Hera's temple by the sea to the west of the city, itself a chaos of construction now, as Polycrates orders it to be entirely rebuilt to new, more splendidly magnificent and sumptuous dimensions. The ancient city walls, too, are being enlarged and strengthened, with square towers planned to go up at strategic points.

It is a building boom for stone-masons. The air is filled with dust and shouting, as huge cut stones are loaded onto carts and trundled up the mountainside, or down to the harbour. There, the extension to the harbour wall is nearly finished. When completed, it will be the largest in the known world, a wonder in itself, providing shelter for the tyrant's vast fleet of fighting ships, the source and the guarantee of his prosperity and power.

With such a rapidly growing population, water is still scarce in the city. The fountains are running low again and rain is needed to refill the cisterns. But it is summer and, again, it has not rained for months. The weather is hot; tempers are growing short and arguments break out among the artisans and slave-owners. This is something Polycrates will have to look to quickly; he has plenty of enemies among the former nobles and aristocrats of Samos, only too ready to exploit any signs of renewed discontent amongst the townspeople.

People go down to the harbour to hear news of the world outside, from incoming trading ships. There are rumours of more movement in far off lands to the east, as the armies of Cyrus, the Persian king, roll ever westward towards the Mediterranean.

Croesus, King of the Lydians, famed for his fabulous wealth, has it in mind to check this Persian expansion if he can, say the reports. The kingdom of Lydia includes most of the Greek cities of Asia Minor, and the Lydians have a long-standing treaty of friendship with the Ionian islanders, including Samos.

Croesus, from the fabulous city of Sardis, has sent to Delphi to enquire of Apollo's oracle there, whether he should undertake the campaign against Persia? To win the favour of Apollo, he has made the most magnificent sacrifice: three thousand animals slaughtered and burnt, couches overlaid with gold and silver, golden cups, tunics and other richly coloured garments burnt with them, and every Lydian has been commanded to contribute a sacrifice according to his means. One hundred and seventeen gold ingots, a golden lion, two huge mixing bowls, one of gold and one of silver... the rumours go on and on.

Surely, with such gifts as these, the Oracle will return a favourable answer? And so it seems, for the Oracle has replied that if Croesus attacks the Persians, he will destroy an empire.

Just to make sure, Croesus has contracted another alliance, with the Spartans, requesting that they should come to his help if he should need it. To seal this pact, the Spartans send a beautiful and costly bronze bowl to Croesus, but it never reaches Sardis. The sea route from Sparta to the Anatolian coast just happens to go past Samos; the Spartan ship is intercepted by pirates and the bowl disappears.

The Samians deny the theft, they say the Spartans must have sold it to someone, but there is much laughter down at the harbour as this story goes around. Back in Sparta, the insult is bitterly resented and will not be forgotten.

Then, a few weeks later, comes terrible news. Croesus has been defeated and the Persians have taken Sardis. Harpagon the Mede brought camels into the front line of battle, which no cavalry horse can endure, so Croesus' cavalry was routed and the city besieged. The Spartans found that, unfortunately, they had not the time to come to the help of their allies after all, so all has been lost. Croesus is now King Cyrus' slave, and Cyrus is near the shores of the Aegean. One by one, the cities of Lydia are taken, their crops destroyed and their people massacred or enslaved. The islanders are no longer laughing. Terrible rumours are spreading about the appalling cruelty of the barbarians.

And what of the Oracle's prediction? The Gods shrug their shoulders. An empire has indeed been destroyed, just as predicted. It is Croesus' fault if he did not realise that it would be his own.

*

Polycrates sits in the luxurious splendour of his palace, and considers his options. His spies tell him that the Persians are unlikely to press further westwards, out into the Aegean. They prefer to wage war on land, being fearsome horsemen but indifferent sailors. It would be wise to send presents instead to Amasis, Pharoah of Egypt. He knows that Amasis is afraid of a Persian attack, and would be favourable towards a naval strategy in which he and his allies control the waves. If Cyrus could not attack Egypt by sea, then he would be unlikely to attack it at all, as his army would be vulnerable while trying to negotiate the waterless northern coast of the Sinai desert.

So overtures are made, and presents exchanged, and the alliance is sealed. Amasis has agreed to pay a great deal of money for this protection: eight tons of silver per year, an enormous sum. Polycrates uses it to build up a navy of no less than one hundred galleys, each with fifty oars: his famous *pentekonters*. With his force of a thousand bowmen he is now hugely powerful, and Samos continues to prosper.

War: there was always war, of course, if not with Persia, then with Miletus, or Phocaea, Corinth or Sparta, or with the tyrant's own rebellious exiles. But war on this scale is highly profitable to Samos, in weakening her commercial rivals, and

Polycrates enjoys being spoken of as 'the most magnificent of tyrants.'

And the Gods still seem to favour him. As Polycrates had gambled, the Great King chooses not to press further west into the Aegean. Instead, leaving Harpagon to control Lydia, Cyrus turns back eastwards, towards the steppes of Central Asia, taking his vast armies to subdue the tribes of the east, from the Hindu Kush to the Aral Sea. For the next few years the islanders will be safe, at least until Cyrus dies and is succeeded by his eldest son. And when that happens, it is towards Egypt that the new King of Persia will turn his attention.

*

IV

A DISAPPOINTMENT

Victor Guérin diligently wrote up his notes on his archaeological investigations. He liked to do this sitting at his window, every morning, early, before the household woke up. The sun was not yet too hot; the cicadas not yet too noisy, and the olive tree outside his window threw a partial shade. Sparrows twittered and tumbled in the dust outside. In the cool of his room, a cockroach made its way slowly across his writing table, towards the ink-stand.

His pages were covered with the careful strokes of his beautiful copperplate hand, large and deliberate, in contrast to his small, energetic self. Each time the packet of papers reached a certain quantity, they would be parcelled up and sent off to his publishers, by donkey down to the port, then by ship to Athens, then overland by courier to Paris.

His mood this morning was cross. "The village of Tigani" he wrote "which consists of no more than a dozen houses, is entirely constructed out of ancient materials and, under the layer of mud and chalk with which they have been plastered, one finds beautiful slabs of marble which have been broken up and mutilated. I found, in the wall of a miserable cafe, some lovely Ionic columns and, inside a shop, a funerary stele, ornamented with elegant bas-relief, being used as a doorstop!

It is the hand of Man, even more than Time, which has destroyed these monuments. The history of Samos tells us that the island has been repeatedly ravaged and its treasures carted off, but its own people have completed the destruction. They have ploughed up the foundations of the town, to grow vegetables."

"What is more" he continued "I have searched in vain for the *agora*, the central meeting place of the ancient city, on the basis of a passage from Plutarch. And indeed, in 1822, when work was begun on the foundations of the fort which now occupies the promontory to the west of Tigani, a number of important inscriptions were found. However, I am unable to consult these inscriptions myself, because they were seized and taken away by the Turks, a dozen years ago, and Mr Lycurgus' house, where these inscriptions were kept, as well as a great number of other fragments of sculptures and ancient bas-reliefs, lost all its treasures, which the Ottoman government has quite simply taken away.

"The confusion is total. Continuing westwards, through the lower part of the old town, one stumbles repeatedly over lovely fragments of marble; walls and arches of Roman construction lie where they have fallen, beside or on top of the remains of Hellenic buildings, and I have observed a number of important ruins dating from the Roman era, which have Hellenic foundations. All of this, in general, is in a state of such disorder that it is practically impossible to define the shape and size of the monuments of which this rubble is all that remains.

If one climbs northwards, up to the high part of the town, one finds the same chaos and confusion, confusion which increases every year, so that to the eye of the observer, it becomes more and more impossible to establish the original configuration of the great city this used to be.

Almost the entire site, in fact, is now divided up into small plots, planted with vines or patches of wheat, and separated by walls or, rather, by piles of ancient marble of all kinds, which each peasant has picked up in his field, and piled up around the edges, both to clear the interior and to mark its boundaries.

How, then, can one hope, in the midst of such displaced and muddled material, to put together, today, the layout and in some way the physiognomy of this famous city?"

Monsieur Guérin sighed, and put down his pen. He blotted his page, as the cockroach scurried hastily under the table. It was of no use, really, he knew. He had tried to talk to some of the farmers himself, with absolutely no result. Maybe he could talk to the Governor, an educated man who was, after all, himself a native of Samos. It would be necessary to interest the entire island in the conservation of these precious remains, he thought, and then to get the island's General Assembly to pass a law putting the whole area into some sort of national ownership. Of course, he added hurriedly, to himself, an indemnity would have to be accorded to each peasant for the loss of his land.

What nonsense! It could never be done. He pushed back his chair, squashing the cockroach as he did so, and stepped out into the morning sunshine.

*

Meeting the Governor and his family at breakfast later, Monsieur Guerin carefully put forward his proposal. He suggested that, at least, the fields containing the remains of the great Temple of the Goddess Hera might be protected and taken into ownership by the island's General Assembly, this being both one of the most important and the most endangered of the ancient monuments. He himself, with the Governor's permission, would undertake an archaeological investigation of the site. Did the Governor think such an idea might be workable?

The Governor did not wish to offend his guest, but he was considerably embarrassed by the request. The Turkish Protectorate, which he represented, had no interest in showcasing the glories of ancient Greece. There would be no funds forthcoming for such a project and, probably, little interest at the General Assembly, either. Clapping his guest on the shoulder, however, he promised he would propose it himself, at the next available opportunity. He would also be happy to provide his guest with a sufficient number of convicts and their guards, as labourers for the digging, if that would be useful. Meanwhile, if he wished – why not? – the Governor saw no objection to the gentleman opening negotiations with the farmers who owned the fields, as long as this would be at his own expense.

*

I confess, I was very excited at the idea. This was just the sort of project I knew I would enjoy. There would be opportunities to explore the marshland flora, and to make drawings, if the Governor's wife could spare me. The older lady looked disapproving; I saw that my enthusiasm could have seemed somehow suspicious. However, there could hardly be anything inappropriate in my accompanying such a gentleman as Monsieur Guerin, could there?

She nodded briefly. I was pleased to see that my teacher stroked his small moustache with satisfaction.

*

Some days later, we left the outskirts of the village of Chora, to visit a farmer. The donkey which accompanied us was laden with excavating tools and hessian bags. We were on our way to the *Heraion*, the great temple of Hera, wife of Zeus. I knew the temple well. I remembered, as a child, playing amongst the huge, warm stones, scrambling over columns fallen in the grass, little girls skipping from one to the next, and running races, plaits flying, to see who could reach the far end of the temple, but never reaching it, so far away did it stretch. We children climbed, and jumped from the top of the great high sacrificial altar, and slept, tired out, in the shade of the vast marble column bases, watched over by the Goddess Hera, mother of us all. It was a place I loved.

"If there is one island in the Archipelago which offers to the traveller, in its great and austere landscape, such masculine and severe beauty in the shape and contours of its mountains, it assuredly must be the island of Samos" declaimed Guérin, as we made their way westwards, along the track which led to the *Heraion*.

"And indeed, there is something masculine and energetic in the nature of the Samian people which, depending on the circumstances, can produce either brigands or heroes. The mountainous nature of their island, their tradition of battling the sea in all weathers, their unending struggle against the Turks, all these have printed upon their character a certain *je ne sais quoi* of pride and courage." Monsieur was in expansive and generous mood this morning.

We had passed a number of small shops and hovels along the way, largely constructed, in fact, of pieces of marble taken from the temple, but luckily Monsieur Guérin was enjoying himself, and refused to let the beauty of the day be spoiled.

Did I know, he asked me, that as well as the architect Rhoikos, the famous Theodoros, architect of the *Artemisium*, the great temple of Artemis at Ephesus, had also worked here? Strabo writes that the temple was *hypaethretic*, that is to say, open to the sky in the centre. Herodotus just tells us that it was the largest temple he had ever seen. And indeed, it is quite astonishingly huge: larger even than the Parthenon in Athens.

"And yet" he gestured grandly "of this vast temple, what remains today? One single column, and even that is not complete, as it is lacking two or three drums, as well as its capital. This one remaining column has been damaged by cannon balls fired from the direction of the sea, when the Turks, thinking that such a great column must be full of gold and silver, had tried to bring it down by cannon fire. Can one imagine such ignorance?"

I hardly heard him. I saw the bright poppies growing in the ditches, and the sweet greenness of vines and figs in the fields behind the low walls. I did fear that my tutor was going to be disappointed in his quest, and I was sorry for him, so quixotic in his enthusiasm, so bright and quick and optimistic. He deserved better than the reception which I feared he would get at the hands of the "masculine and energetic" Samian peasant farmers.

And indeed, when we arrived at the large field dotted with broken marble which was our destination, Monsieur Guérin's disappointment was terrible. The negotiations, which he thought had been agreed, appeared to be nothing but moonshine. The owner declared himself very willing to let him dig around in his field, but insisted that he had rented him the field, not its contents. These would remain his property. Of course, he was looking forward to having much beautiful marble uncovered, which he could sell at a profit. He might even start digging up more of it himself.

"In other words", cried Monsieur Guérin, in despair, "everything we find one day will have disappeared the next, and soon there will be nothing left of this temple, for every piece of marble will be taken away as soon as we have uncovered it."

Upon returning to Chora, we learned that the Governor had been called away to Constantinople on urgent business and would not return for many weeks. No proposals had been made, and in his absence nothing could be done. Guérin threw his hat on the floor and went to sit in the garden. *Scélérats!*

I followed him out, slowly, thinking of the texts I had been reading.

"Herodotus tells us there were *three* great marvels in Samos", I reminded him. "There were the harbour mole and the great temple, but the greatest of them all, he tells us, was the tunnel built through the mountain, to bring water to the city in its time of need".

"Ah yes, my dear" he answered me sadly, "but the whereabouts of that, of course, as you know, is lost.

*

V

POLITICS AND POWER

To my disappointment, Monsieur Guerin was not in the mood for history lessons for a while, although I tried, repeatedly, to raise the subject of the tunnel again whenever I found him alone.

"At least, tell me more about those people who lived here all those years ago", I begged him until at last, his vanity piqued by my insistence, I suppose, he graciously agreed to resume our conversations in the garden. We sat, again, in the shade of the fig tree, bright sunlight glancing off the glassy surface of the sea in the distance.

"Of course," he explained carefully, "you will understand that I, as an archaeologist, am more concerned with the material remains to be found here, but I see that you need to know the background to what happened and, in particular, how it was that this island of Samos rose to such prominence such a long time ago.

"As I explained before, this Polycrates was a politician *par excellence*, an expert in arranging alliances, or so he thought. He was not, however, the only expert politician in this area, in the 6th century BC. Let us look again, for instance at the role of Egypt in all of this. And if you wish, we will also look at the reason why this tunnel, which is now lost, was to become so important."

Leaning back in his chair he placed his fingertips together and began. I made sure that he observed the way I hung on to his every word.

EGYPT, ABOUT 535 BC

Amasis, Pharoah of Egypt, sends greetings to Polycrates of Samos. Having heard of Samos' increasing power and fortune, the Pharaoh is interested to find out whether his alliance with Polycrates against the Persian threat would still be to Egypt's advantage. As tyrants, they are well matched, these two. Amasis is as cunning as his new friend and knows very well where his own advantage lies. He is no more nobly born than Polycrates, and every bit as unscrupulous.

He had been an officer in the Egyptian army, who rode to power on the back of a soldiers' revolt against the former Pharoah, Apries. Sent out by Apries to quell the revolt, he instead turned the soldiers against their master. Apries was defeated and the soldiers proclaimed Amasis Pharoah in his place.

Loving pleasure and fond of jokes, he has had a gold footbath, which he and his guests washed their feet in, melted down and made into a statue of one of the Gods, and this he has set up in the city, where the Egyptians treat it with profound reverence. He loves to point out that this is the same footbath in which they used to wash their feet, and pissed and vomited. His own case is much the same, he says, as he was once low born but is now their king, so they had better pay honour and respect to him too, just as they revere the transformed footbath.

Yet, like Polycrates, he is popular among his subjects, for his reign is a time of unexampled prosperity for Egypt, where rich harvests have brought good living for many years. He has introduced a custom which interests Polycrates, by which every man once a year should declare before the provincial governor, the source and the amount of his livelihood. Anyone failing to do this is punished by death.

To the goddess Hera in Samos he has sent two likenesses of himself in wood, to be displayed in the great Heraion temple. These are a mark of his great friendship towards Polycrates, ruler of Samos. This special relationship will protect them both, for a while, from the Persian menace.

But, just like Polycrates, to make sure, Amasis continues to foster guest-friendships and gift-giving with other Greek states: Miletus, Rhodes, and even Sparta, even though he is well aware that such diplomatic feelers will not be well received by Polycrates. It will do no harm, he thinks, if the Samian tyrant finds he is not entirely sure where he stands.

All of mainland Ionia now pays tribute to Cyrus the Persian king, but not Samos. Polycrates pays no tribute to anyone, but plunders the Persian ships instead. Hera's temple fills with costly and beautiful objects seized by Samian pirates who control the shipping lanes between Ionia and the islands. They will steal anything, from anybody: Persians, Lydians, Egyptians, Spartans; no one is safe.

Having no wish to support other alliances, they even steal a gift which was being sent by Amasis to the Spartans: a marvellously woven linen corselet embroidered with golden threads, of a most intricate and valuable kind.

"The Spartans must have sold it to someone," they protest, and there is more laughter down at the harbour. What business does Amasis have with the Spartans, giving them gifts? Polycrates takes careful note.

Samian ships dominate the Aegean and the island grows richer and richer. The famous poets, Ibycus and Anacreon, sing the tyrant's praises; he is hugely popular. But surely this cannot last; there must be a price to pay?

King Cyrus of Persia may be busy elsewhere for a while, and Amasis may choose to overlook such insults for the moment, but the Spartans and the Corinthians will not. Sparta has always aspired to control the Peloponese and be the principal state of Hellas, so Polycrates' naval power poses a real threat to Spartan hegemony. Sparta and Corinth will soon form an alliance.

Neither are things as safe as they seem at home. Polycrates suspects (and he is right) that there is a faction still loyal to the old nobility, which would like to see him brought down. In the old days, before the coup, ties had been close between Sparta and the Samian nobility. The tyrant knows that the Spartans have sent out their spies. He knows that they are in touch with the Samian exiles.

Tyrants have duties, in return for the privileges they enjoy. They must keep their subjects prosperous, and they must give them a sense of security, or they may see themselves ousted. The city walls are impregnable, but the town would be vulnerable to a prolonged siege, because it is so short of water. Polycrates orders his staff to find the very best engineer, to look into the problem, and to offer the very highest rates of pay.

*

THE ENGINEER

In Megara, on the Greek mainland, between Corinth and Attica, there lives a young man who, people all agree, is destined to have a great future.

Having been found to be clever beyond his years, his father has sent him, as a boy, to Miletus to study with the philosophers, so as to learn all that could be learned about the nature of the universe, mathematics, geometry and architecture.

Young Eupalinos sits at the feet of his teachers, devouring all that he is told. He is intrigued by the work of Thales, the Miletian cosmologist, who rejects the old-fashioned beliefs of mythology to explain the physical nature of things. Science cannot be based on the supernatural. Matter is the only principal of all things: all objects have a *nature*, which makes them behave in a particular way, even if this nature has been shaped and created in the mind of the Gods.

The young man is the son of Naustrophos, himself something of an engineer, having had a hand in the construction of a number of large-scale building works on the Peloponesian mainland. At his birth, the boy was given the portentous name of Eupalinos, which means '*One who brings things to a successful conclusion*', but as he grows older, Eupalinos is at a loss to know whether such a name might turn out to be a blessing or a curse. He is aware that it might lead to the setting up of false hopes, and he is wary of accusations of overweening pride.

For these reasons, he works hard at his studies, and even harder when he returns to Megara, on the mainland, as his father's assistant so that over the years, the two of them become well-known and highly recommended as efficient and innovative architects, engineers and designers. They successfully complete a tunnel to bring the water of the Sithnidian nymphs to the palace of Theogenes, the tyrant of Megara. The water flows into a large and beautiful fountain, ornamented and set about by many columns, and Theogenes is pleased.

Eupalinos now has an assistant of his own, who acts as his apprentice and general servant. This boy is the orphaned son of one of the maids in his father's household, and the other women shake their heads, telling stories of how, as a new-born baby, he sat up and spoke to his mother in a strange tongue, just before she died. He is a solitary boy, preferring to play alone, talking and singing to himself or to the trees, sometimes frowning and making fierce gestures at unknown opponents. For this, he has been named Amoun, 'the hidden one'. Eupalinos, a somewhat shy and solitary young man himself, has chosen the boy for his quick intelligence, and for his interest in all things natural.

When the summons from Samos comes, a summons so peremptory it cannot be ignored, it is initially for Naustrophos. The older man, though, sees it as a great chance for his only son, and recommends him in his stead. So Eupalinos sets out on board a ship bound for the eastern seas, taking Amoun with him.

The boy is fascinated by the movement of the water beneath them, spending the long days leaning far out over the prow of the boat, watching the ripple and flow, and calling in delight at the dolphins which leap beside them. Sheerwaters skim across the very tips of the waves, as gusts of wind pour across the water like blown glass and Amoun shouts that far below he can see long-necked dragons dip and plunge, their tails slapping foam, their monstrous heads black and shiny. The sailors laugh indulgently. They grow fond of the lad, saying that he is a lucky omen.

And it seems that maybe they are right, for as the bright light dances on the water, the wind blows them south-eastward at a good pace. The ship calls in at every island on the way, Salamis, Aigina, then south-east down to Kea, Siros and finally heads for Delos.

*

All has been clear sailing until now, but suddenly there is a sharp thunderclap. The wind veers suddenly to the north so that the boat is flung off course as the sky grows dark, split by lightning. The air is alive with thunderous rain, the winds are spitting and snarling, the mast ropes flail about, screaming through the air and whipping against the sail, and the ship's timbers crack and shiver. It is a pandemonium of noise.

The sailors struggle with the rigging and the helmsman yells for more oarsmen as the boat heaves and swings and the wind grows stronger. Suddenly, they see huge craggy cliffs rearing above them, holed all over with caves, deep and black. Stalactites hang down from the lip like sharp teeth and, from below, sharp-edged rocks rise up from the sea, as if to meet them.

The captain curses and swears as the helmsman tries to hold the steering oar, for this is the island of Ophiousa, famous for its hundreds of serpents. The sailors raise their hands to Heaven, screaming and begging for mercy.

"Great Poseidon, save us, for we do not mean to offend you" shouts Eupalinos in alarm; to be on the safe side he also mutters a prayer to Helios, great Apollo, in the name of all that is beautiful, to help them. And, at last, the wind does begin to die and the angry waves to subside. They are swept, after many hours, past the tip of the island and carried on out again, into the open sea.

Amoun has shown no fear during all of this, but sits still in the prow of the boat, humming and whistling his queer little tunes. When at last they see the island of Delos before them, they limp into harbour for repairs. They are detained in Delos for many days.

Here, Eupalinos learns more about the tyrant who is to be his new master. He discovers that one of Polycrates' most recent conquests was the small island of Rhenia, off the coast of Delos. Having subdued the few inhabitants there, the tyrant attached the island by a silver chain to Delos, and announced with great fanfare that he has thereby made an offering to Apollo.

It is an impressive statement, and Eupalinos notes it well. He, too, takes the opportunity to make an offering to Apollo on this sacred island, and to pray for a successful outcome to their journey. He is a man of science, it is true, but at the same time, he is not so foolish as to risk offending the Gods who, he still believes, must have shaped and created the universe itself. So, perhaps, he shows himself to be a wise man, as he will find he will need all the help he can summon, in the years to come.

At last the boat is repaired and the wind changes, so they can head north-east to Icaria and, finally, after many days, to Samos. Eupalinos whistles in astonishment on seeing the vast great harbour, so full of ships, and the size of the town with its many grand buildings. It is a relief to step out onto the great harbour wall after so many days at sea, but the sailors are sorry to lose Amoun. They say that his songs must have pleased the mermaids or trytons or other creatures which live beneath the ocean, and so assured their safety.

*

Eupalinos and Amoun are met at the harbour by Polycrates' steward, and taken up to the palace, where the tyrant is waiting for them. The hall is crowded with courtiers trying to attract the tyrant's attention, but the steward pushes them through the crowd to where Polycrates is seated, like a king on his throne, surrounded by his special favourites.

Eupalinos looks at this famously violent and powerful ruler, and sees that he is big and fleshy, with soft red lips nestled in the thick of his black beard. Polycrates sees a tall, thin, awkward young man, with a small boy hiding behind him. He fingers his beard carefully, and wonders. He has been impressed with Eupalinos' credentials and the recommendations he has heard, but above all he is impressed with his name, which he takes as the most excellent of omens.

He makes sure Eupalinos understands what a high rate of pay he will be getting, then sweetly suggests that the boy might like to stay in the palace for a time, while the Engineer begins his survey. Eupalinos replies curtly that Amoun is his apprentice and will be needed. The tyrant frowns; he is not used to being refused.

"Well now," he says, turning to his crowd of favourites "What kind of manners are these?" The courtiers titter nervously; no-one can be sure what will happen next.

A pudgy little girl runs up to sit on the tyrant's knee; this is Parthenope, his little daughter. She is richly dressed, and her eyes are heavily made up. She sticks her tongue out at Amoun; the boy blushes furiously and this makes the courtiers roar with laughter. Polycrates shrugs, laughs derisively, pats his little daughter's head and dismisses the engineer with a wave. Eupalinos tries to hurry the boy away; the throng of courtiers giggle and stare at them as they turn to leave. This has not been a good start.

*

VI

THEN LET US FIND IT

"IF IT IS LOST, then let us find it" I said firmly. I was not yet
willing to put aside the question of the lost tunnel.

It was very hot. The Governor had still not returned
after several days' absence in Constantinople and his wife
had retired to her bedroom with the blinds drawn and a cold
compress over her eyes. Sighing, Monsieur Guérin assured me
that he had already researched the question of the tunnel, but
that he had been able to elicit only vague and contradictory
information from the local inhabitants. He pulled out his
notebook, and read to me:

"As soon as I arrived on this island, I questioned
several inhabitants of Chora and Tigani, concerning the
whereabouts of the remains of this ancient aqueduct. They
pointed out to me a number of large caves, into which I
penetrated, but I realized at once that they in no way
resembled Herodotus' description and none could ever
have served as a water channel. Some of them, indeed, were
close to the ruins of the lovely Roman bridge-aqueduct
which crosses behind Mt Kastro, and it was clear that
my informants thought I was referring to this, although,

obviously, it dates to several centuries later than that described by Herodotus.

I entered cave after cave surrounding Mt Kastro, and also those of Mt Katarouga, but I quickly convinced myself that it was vain to search there for our tunnel, and that I was quite wrong to rely on the writings of previous scholars, illustrious though they may be, some of whom even maintain that the Eupalinos tunnel cuts through the mountain between Mytilini and Chora, bringing water to the town via this same (Roman) bridge!"

Here Monsieur Guérin allowed himself to smile a little at the unbelievable ignorance of others. Wiping his face with his handkerchief, he shook his head and laid down his notebook.

I thought hard for a moment, then dared to say: "Herodotus writes that the mountain was nine hundred feet high, so this must surely be Mt Kastro?" With a nod, my companion allowed that it must.

"When I was little" I told him dreamily, "we sometimes used to walk up to the monastery over there, where the old monks would give us pomegranates to suck. Over the other side of the mountain the land is fertile, full of orchards and flowers. If you continue over the ravine, you come across a little chapel there, called St John or *Agios Ioannis*, nowadays called *Ayanni*. There is a spring of water nearby, where we used to drink and dip our toes in and splash our faces; it was always so beautifully cold. All the local farmers use this source, and I have always heard that it is the most copious spring of water around here."

Guérin looked at me carefully over his spectacles. "The village of Ayanni is rather a long way behind the mountain, don't you think?" he asked kindly. "However, I would like to visit this monastery you mention, for interest, and perhaps the little chapel, too."

*

Over the following days we wandered around and about the fringes of Mount Kastro and climbed up to the monastery of Moni Panagias Spillianis again. We sat in the cool, earthy dampness of the grotto behind the church there, and another old monk brought us olives and hard, yellow cheese, with cold water to drink, and sat with us for a while.

Refreshed and filled once more with enthusiasm, Guerin suggested we climb up to the old acropolis again, if I was not too tired. Too tired indeed! I was happier than I could remember being for a long time, thinking of the contribution I was making by acting as my tutor's guide. I had always known these old stones but had never, until now, put them into context. Now I perceived that Guerin could do this for me; I felt as though I had found a willing fount of information, and would drink it dry if I could. Besides, I had just remembered something which I thought Monsieur Guerin ought to see.

"Come," I said, "let me show you."

We passed the mighty, ancient, looming walls we had explored before and arrived at last, breathless and hot, on the vast plateau high above. The bumpy ground here was covered with low, spiny bushes and rocks, full of the broken stones of ancient houses, now thickly overgrown. We came upon four huge, square cisterns, several metres deep, cut into the living rock to catch rainfall, but now almost filled up with stones and earth. Not far from there, I showed him a peculiar hole in the ground, blocked by rocks at the entrance and extremely narrow, but immensely deep.

I told him: "The shepherd boys who used to herd their goats up here, when I was little, would drop stones down this hole and try to count the seconds before they heard the stones reach the bottom. None of them were ever able to work it out, the hole was so deep."

I was extremely pleased by the extravagance of his reaction. "Good Heavens, ma chere Eleni,!" he shouted, so loudly that some nearby crows flew up in alarm, and I jumped in surprise, myself, but he was merely peering down into this 'curious abyss', as he described it later. "What can one make of this? Is it the work of nature or of man?"

Later on he showed me his notes, written up when we returned to Chora.:

" If I had been able to examine it properly," he wrote, "I would have been able to ascertain whether it was a sort of artificial well, or simply another of those mysterious crevasses which appear in these parts. But the hole in the top is so small that the eye can distinguish nothing, although one can feel air rising from within which is cooler than the surrounding air.

"I suspect, however, that it is indeed man-made, quite possibly a shaft corresponding in some way with Eupalinos' underground tunnel, as it seems to lie more or less in that direction. If this is the case, its depth must be at least 180 metres."

I wonder whether this was perhaps the moment when it occurred to him that he might be on the cusp of some new discovery? This was so very important to him. For myself, the delight was in the possibility of new knowledge; for Monsieur Guerin, I am afraid, it was all the thought of his own importance and renown.

We were alone in the centre of this extraordinary acropolis, high up on its mountain. No-one ever seemed to climb up this far, as we had done, and yet I thought it most beautiful.

There was nothing but a great, vast silence, except for the wind, and the distant mewling of seagulls in the rocks below. The sun almost blinded us and the heat was exhausting, but the wind dried the perspiration on our faces as we stood and stared at the view all around us, realising that we could see in every direction, over hills and valleys to the north and west, and sea to the south. To the east, across the straits, the coast of Turkey was so clear that we could even make out buildings and roads.

I led him across the stony ground towards the northern walls of the acropolis, from where we could see the fragrant, fertile valley beyond. The contrast was striking: all so brown and dry on the southern, seaward side of the mountain, and so green and fruitful in the valley below.

"There is the water" I pointed, "it must have come from somewhere over there". Guerin could not but agree, but the question was, where? Looked at from such a height, the valley seemed impossibly far away.

"Herodotus clearly states that the tunnel *through the mountain* was 'seven stades long', which is about one mile, over a thousand metres. That is extraordinarily long for a tunnel at that time; it could hardly have been longer. How would the water, wherever it was, have reached the start of the tunnel?"

Of course, he was unwilling to admit that I might be right, having dismissed my suggestion so summarily when I first made it, but he had to admit that it might be a good idea to have a look at the 'copious spring' I had mentioned, at Agios Ioannis, or Ayanni or Aiyades or whatever it was called these days.

*

The Governor had still not returned, but the local military commander, Mr Alexis, came to call on Monsieur Guérin, whom he insisted on calling 'Professor'. He had heard, he said that the Professor was interested in archaeology, as indeed he was himself. The Governor had mentioned that he might be in need of some labourers. Could he perhaps be of assistance? A number of convicts were at the moment languishing in the prison at Chora, in need of useful occupation. He would be happy, he said with a wave of his hand, to put them at the Professor's disposition, along with a sufficient number of soldiers for their security, of course. What was the Professor working on at the moment?

Monsieur was not at all willing to tell the Commander about his failure at the Heraion temple. Carefully putting his fingers together and leaning back in his chair, he spoke instead of the tunnel described by Herodotus, of the lack of awareness of the locals of their own heritage, and of the erroneous writings of former scholars on the subject. However, when he mentioned, with a little laugh, the 'crevasse' I had shown him, and my story of a 'copious spring' (Herodotus' own words) on the other side of the mountain, the Commander nodded his head.

"Ah yes", he said, "I believe that a long time ago, there used to be a large hole by that spring, which the farmers have since blocked up. How amusing if that should turn out to be the entrance to your tunnel".

A 'copious spring', and a large hole next to it! Monsieur Guérin could hardly contain himself. Shaking the Commander by the hand and thanking him profusely, and calling to me to come at once, it was decided that we would all three set out the next day to inspect the crevasse, the chapel, the spring and the blocked-up hole. If, as we all hoped, it proved to be worthwhile, the Commander would bring up his convict prisoners and work could be commenced forthwith.

Imagine: to be the first archaeologist to be able to prove the existence of Eupalinos' tunnel… Victor Guérin slept very little that night. He thought hard of publication and fame, but also of the dear young lady whose intelligent help was so useful to him, and whose enthusiasm and energy were so inspiring.

Bon Dieu! He believed he was actually beginning to count on her! The very thought made him stroke his moustache again, even to twirl it at the ends.

*

VII

WATER

I am nothing if not a practical person. That evening I retired to my room to look again at my books and re-read Herodotus' description of the sheer size of this tunnel we were looking for. "*A tunnel nearly a mile long, eight feet high and eight feet wide, driven clean through the base of a hill nine hundred feet in height. The whole length of it carries a second cutting thirty feet deep and three broad...*"

But how on earth would it have been done, with none of the modern equipment available to construction workers in our own time? And, I supposed, no modern means of measurement either. I knew that the ancients were wonderful architects, who apparently did build their temples with no modern equipment, but surely this tunnel was on another scale of difficulty altogether. I would have to ask my tutor for his ideas on just how such an extraordinary feat of engineering could have been achieved.

As we climbed the mountain early next morning, Monsieur Guerin was happy to expand. "Picture it to yourself" he told me. "Think about what it all looked like in those days, on just such an early morning as this."

A cock crows in the early dawn, then another, and another. Clear, imperious, insistent, the sound carries across the hills in the pale grey morning light. The cockerels vie with each other, each one desperate to be heard above the rest, all striving to be top of the dung heap.

A path winds upwards, from the edge of the city, up the mountainside to where men are already at work in the distance, placing the foundations of the tower which will guard the north-western side of the city walls. Eupalinos climbs steadily up the mountain side towards the tower, Amoun trotting beside him, the slave following, carrying the bundle of cut poles which they will use as marker rods. It is a long, hard climb. They greet the men as they pass, and continue on upwards through thorny bush and scrub, till they reach, at last, a point where they can see over and down the northern side, inland, away from the sea shore, down towards vineyards and rich olive groves and the wide, fertile valley beyond. It is a path which will soon become well worn with use.

The tyrant's orders had been imperious, insistent. Like the cockerels, thinks Amoun, in disgust. The work must begin immediately. Bring water into the city, from the copious springs in the valley on the other side of the mountain. Bring it round the mountain, or bring it through, the tyrant does not care, but that part of the work which will lie outside the city walls must be hidden, or it will be vulnerable, easily cut off or the water poisoned by a besieging enemy. It is a heavy responsibility, and Eupalinos can think of no precedent to help him in his design.

Amoun looks down into the valley so far below, and begins to laugh. "Water only runs downhill" he chants, and grins up at his master. Eupalinos sits down to rest, and gazes around, at the well-watered valley to the north, the dry city and the sea to the south, and the mountain in between. Should they go round the mountain, or through it? Round would be a great deal easier, cutting a canal, necessitating only a covered channel, but it would be much longer, and would be almost impossible to conceal along all of its length. A tunnel straight through the mountain would be much shorter, and more hidden, but his heart almost stops at the thought of it. Great Hera, he thinks, Mother Goddess, to pierce the very centre of your mountain! The sheer size of the task appals him; it is a work of Titans, not of men. He has dug tunnels before, but never on this scale.

The boy has wandered off to look for berries, and the slave has fallen asleep under a tree. Up there, where they are sitting, the sun is hot overhead, and the wind is strong, rippling as it blows through long, waving grass, just as it ripples in waves over the sea, just as water ripples when it flows.

Eupalinos closes his eyes, and sees cold, fresh water flowing fast under rock. Concentrating hard, he sees an ancient Titan goddess, wild haired Tethys, wife of Oceanus, and her daughters, the streams and rivers, bright children among the goddesses, who all alike look after the earth and the depths of the standing water. So he prays to the old Mother, source of fountains, and also to Poseidon, Earth-shaker, who can split mountains. He knows that if he concentrates hard enough an idea will come to him.

He has been summoned here on the basis of his reputation as a problem solver. And he tells himself he is a tunneller, not a canal digger. Such a work would be huge, and he has no idea, yet, how he could establish either the direction or the level of a tunnel for which there is no point from where he can actually see the position where both ends should eventually lie... but his mind's eye has shown him a vision of water spurting from the rock face, cascading down an inevitable gradient, down to the level of the sea.

He feels his excitement mounting at the challenge and, calling Amoun, he grips the boy's shoulder as he gets to his feet. A tunnel it will have to be. They start down the other side of the mountain, and the boy crows out aloud like the cockerel as he breaks into a run.

In the valley, at Ayanni, they find the large and copious spring, placed there by another kindly god. The water gushes out through two mouths cut into huge marble slabs put there before anyone can remember, when gods still walked the earth and men were giants. The boy cups his hands and brings them water, cold and clear, delicious. Eupalinos turns to look back up to where they have come from.

Between the spring and the mountain they have had to cross two small ravines which must be bridged, before the tunnel can even begin. But this will not do, for bridges cannot be hidden. They will have to begin by canalising the water after all, following the horizontal contours of this hill in two wide curves to make a feed channel, leading to the tunnel mouth. This will not be too difficult, the distance is not too far. He can see it in his mind's eye, a channel cut deep enough so that when covered over it will not show.

But the tunnel itself, where should it start? And where will it finish? How will he fix its direction, how calculate its length, and how will he keep the level right, so that the water, as his boy says, will keep flowing downhill?

Days later, a possible line for the feed channel is marked out, following the contours around the hill above both ravines, to where it reaches the highest possible point in the mountainside where the tunnel mouth could be opened. Eupalinos is satisfied that the spring water will flow down along this level, when the feed-channel is dug.

This is his first mistake.

*

To celebrate the success of the pact with Amasis in Egypt, Polycrates summons back to his court the poet Anacreon. Beautiful Anacreon! A poet of love and wine, he composes his songs with wit and good humour. Rumour has it, that he is one of the lovers of Polycrates; his poems are erotic, full of fun and the glitter of the court. Anacreon is in love with everyone, it seems, or pretends to be, causing much laughter as he sings of hopeless infatuation, or invites his audience to conspire in getting the boys drunk:

I love Cleobulus, I am mad for Cleobulus, I gaze at Cleobulus. O Dionysus, advise Cleobulus well, that he accept my love.

With his songs and poems of the charms of drink and sex, Anacreon brings a new sense of decadence to the entertainment of the *symposion*, with its tables loaded with fine food and flowers, scented garlands and beautiful servants, where, as he sings, 'the lovely gifts of the Muses and Aphrodite are mingled'. 'For my words the boys will all love me' he sighs 'for I sing of grace, I know how to talk with grace'. He sings in metaphors of drunken love, love as a ball game, love as the charioteer, the axe of love, dicing and boxing with love. And he does not sing only for the boys: offering mock prayers to the gods for success in love, he sings of the girl who is a frightened deer, and how he will ride the unbroken filly.

More and more wine is drunk. The partying becomes wild, and drunken and dangerous. A jealous scandal in the court erupts when Anacreon's praise of one of the boys proves too provoking. Polycrates, in anger, orders the boy's long hair cut off, but Anacreon laughs and soothes and makes a joke in self mockery, and the dangerous moment passes.

...you lack the hair, which once shaded your neck in abundance. But now you are smooth-browed, and your hair, falling into rough hands, has tumbled down in a heap, into the black dust. Bravely did it meet the slash of steel but I am wasted away with sorrow. For what can one do...

As fond of women as of men or boys, Polycrates sets up the Samian bazaar in the city: an alley of skilled courtesans, beautiful enough even to vie with the famed brothels of Sardis. It is noised abroad that these flowers of the Samians do indeed outshine the flowers of the Lydians, so that 'luxurious Samos' becomes a byword in all Hellas. In fact, the island is now becoming as famous for the luxury and incontinent enjoyment to be found there, as for war-mongering and piracy.

(All these are details, however, which Monsieur Guérin, hard at work on his texts, does not feel it is necessary to recount to his pupil).

Everything Polycrates does has to be the biggest and the best. The great temple built for Hera by the famous architect Rhoikos is 'the greatest of all known Greek temples', so hugely gigantic in its conception that, in fact, it will never be finished. His ships are the most numerous, his harbour the largest, his acropolis the best defended. Theodoros the artist, Democedes the physician, Rhoikos the architect, poets, musicians, philosophers; all who come to the court of the Samian are the most renowned, the most popular, the greatest and the best.

Hundreds of slaves and prisoners of war have died in the construction of these works, and many more will die before they are finished, but this is of no interest to the tyrant. Yet this is a triumph which cannot last, as Polycrates knows as well as anyone. The Gods are not to be trusted when they appear to favour you too much. They love a joke, and their jokes, too, can be cruel.

*

The political situation is not as rosy as the tyrant's advisors like to make it appear. Polycrates is enormously popular with the common folk, and with the countless hangers-on at court, but there is considerable resentment among some sections of the aristocracy, who are in touch with the exiled former land-owners, and with influential powers in other city states.

Polycrates is no lover of the aristocracy nor, particularly, of the *hoi polloi*. But his popularity depends on his continuing to protect the people from exploitation by that same ruling class, and in ensuring that they have their share in the general prosperity. For this, he is hated by the old aristocracy, even while they attend at court. And there is a cold, sour feeling of fear attached to this attendance, for no one, high or low, dares to risk getting on the wrong side of Polycrates.

Many of the exiled relatives of these aristocratic courtiers have taken refuge in Sparta, with whom they have had a history of friendship over many years. There are offerings at Hera's temple of the famous Spartan bronze cauldrons and statues dedicated by Spartan visitors. Pottery from Sparta is still fashionable, and trade continues in spite of a growing strain in relationships since the tyrant's coup.

For Sparta is not pleased at the sight of Polycrates' success. In Spartan ambition to be recognized as the strongest state in the Aegean, there is no room for a rival. Diplomatic feelers between Sparta and the Samian aristocrats continue to develop in secrecy.

There is one group of aristocratic zealots whom Polycrates finds particularly irritating. They are adherents of a secret politico-religious community led by a philosopher named Pythagoras, a seer, a miracle-worker, a healer, mathematician, astronomer and ascetic. He teaches the inter-connectedness of things: the harmony of the spheres and the use of music for therapeutic ends, the doctrine of the unity of all animate beings, vegetarianism, and the transmigration of souls. His followers even believe him to have supernatural powers, saying that he understands the language of animals, and is able to appear in several places at once. Astonishingly, he has been heard to preach against the excesses of the tyrants' court, and his school is in danger of becoming a focus of discontent, and a rallying point for the tyrants' political opponents.

The Mystic's personal charisma is anathema to Polycrates who would simply have had them all executed if Pythagoras were not so popular with the common folk. But then he decides on a better idea. He sends him into exile, but with a letter of recommendation, to Amasis in Egypt, trusting that Pythagoras will take his troublemaking with him. It makes him smile to think of Amasis having to deal with this nuisance.

This does not work out quite as the tyrant had intended, however, as Pythagoras is welcomed in Egypt, and given the opportunity to share the Egyptian priests' way of life. He is initiated by the priests into all the severity of their mysteries, and becomes the only foreigner ever to be granted the privilege of taking part in their worship of the Egyptian gods. After many months, to the tyrant's fury, he will announce his intention of returning to Samos to continue his teaching.

Polycrates retires to bed, and has appalling dreams. He dreams of the Persians turning once more towards the west, advancing closer and closer, sacking cities, burning and killing, cutting off the ears and noses of their captives. He dreams of Egypt, and the futility of an alliance which gives him much silver, but no military security. He dreams of mysterious Sparta across the sea, arrogant and threatening, sending their cold-eyed spies like spiders to entangle the islanders in their complex diplomatic webs, and the islanders themselves, disloyal and not to be trusted, any of them.

These dreams are common-place; he shrugs them off in his sleep and dreams instead that he is being washed by Zeus himself, and anointed by the sun-god Helios. Soothed now, he turns in his bed, and sleeps peacefully till morning.

Yet trouble is stirring on the Island. Even Anacreon says so. It is clear that there are ambassadors at the court who are playing a double game. Beneath the laughter and glitter there is also mistrust and fear. But among the aristocrats and the courtiers, the undercurrent of tension and distrust is fanned by the universal suspicion that the most skilful player at pitting all sides against the middle, is Polycrates himself.

In Egypt, Amasis, another skilled player at these games, sends Polycrates a letter. Addressed to 'My dear friend and ally', the letter flatters and cajoles, and ends with a warning. The gods are jealous of success, he writes, and Polycrates' excessive prosperity is leading him into danger. He suggests that his friend should make a public display of humility. He should think of whatever it is he values most, whatever it is he would most regret the loss of, and throw it away. Only this, he intones, will placate the Gods and rescue his dear friend from danger.

It is quite clear to Polycrates that Amasis hopes he will publicly renounce some valuable political alliance which will be to the Egyptian's advantage, but he pretends to take the letter at face value. Looking through his treasures, he hits upon a magnificent ring, an emerald set in gold, made for him by Theodoros, *'gift of the gods'*, the artist and co-architect of Hera's temple.

With ceremony and music and dancing, the court crowds into a galley and sails out of Samos harbour, as the townsfolk wave and cheer from the shore. Out in the open sea, Polycrates takes the ring from his finger and, in full view of everyone on board, hurls it into the water. Then they all return to the island, to lament the loss of his treasure.

A few days later, a fisherman arrives at the palace with an enormous fish he has caught, and presents it to the tyrant as a gift. The fish is cooked and brought to table, sliced open and, behold, there is the ring, in its belly!

This time, the whole island, court and commoners, is united in laughter. Many songs and satirical poems are written, praising their invincible tyrant whom the Gods clearly love so much. But Amasis is not amused. He replies that apparently it is impossible for one man to save another from his destiny. The Gods have evidently refused his offering, he says, and he predicts that Polycrates will one day die a miserable death. Therefore it is with regret that he must bring the pact between Polycrates and himself to an end, in order that when the eventual calamity falls he might avoid the distress he would otherwise have felt, had Polycrates still been his friend.

Has Amasis somehow heard something? The tyrant frowns, and sends out more spies.

*

THE TUNNEL MOUTH

High up on the top of Mount Castro, Eupalinos is frowning too. Work has not yet started on the tunnel itself, but is proceeding well on the open conduit from the Ayanni spring to the mountain-side, which will be covered by stone slabs and earth after it is completed. It follows the contour of the valley in a sinuous curve, so that its total length will be nearly three times as long as the direct line but, in this way, it will be able to be completely hidden.

The water must be brought from the spring at Ayanni to the north of the mountain, then to be tunnelled through to a point on the south side which will lie inside the city wall. The water channel must have a slope, but not one too steep, to avoid the water flowing too fast. Therefore, the conduit has to decline between the spring and the tunnel mouth, and the tunnel itself has to be a little lower again. So the level of the tunnel has to be determined at the north end by the level of the conduit, and the level at the south end, where the tunnel will eventually finish, will be determined by the level at the north end.

So far, so good, but how is he to locate this putative exit point at the south end, and fix the direction for tunnelling? Standing on the crest of the mountain, Eupalinos cannot see Ayanni in the north and the seashore to the south at the same time. The slope is too steep and there is too much overhang and too many trees.

The sun is setting, and he notes with irritation that his boy appears to have run off again. He sees him at last high up in a tree where he has climbed in search of birds' nests, but when he calls him he realises that Amoun is using the tree as a look-out, staring intently out in the direction of the coast. The Engineer laughs to himself. This is why he values the boy so much; his quick, bright mind loves problems; if he can, he will work out ways around them in the hope that his master may not yet have thought of them. Eupalinos claps his hands and beckons to the boy to come down. One tree is still not tall enough, he thinks, but if they could build a tower the height of two or maybe three trees…?

The tyrant has allowed him all the men and equipment he may require to construct this thing, as the water problem is becoming crucial. So a wooden tower is built to a height where there is a direct line of sight from Ayanni in the north to the seashore in the south. Then sighting poles are set up on the tower, to align with markers at both ends, and the direction is fixed.

The tunnel should end as near as possible to the city centre, but must be no longer than is necessary, so the line he selects does not cross the steepest peak of the mountain, but passes just below it, to the west, where the profile of the ridge is smoother. More sighting poles are then extended down both sides of the mountain, and the line of the tunnel is established.

As the days go by, the boy is chirruping with pride as he carries the *groma*, Eupalinos' sighting tool, up the mountainside each morning. Starting at the north end, where the tunnel mouth will be, they stick a measuring pole into the ground, then they set off up the mountain, the slaves hammering in more poles as often as is needed to ensure that they can sight horizontally from the top of one pole to the bottom of the next.

Hours later, at the top, Amoun triumphantly places a pole at the highest point. Eupalinos now adds up all the height readings taken from pole to pole up the north side, which gives him a figure for the elevation: the height from the tunnel mouth to the top of the mountain. Starting down the other side, and still following their line of direction previously established, they read off the measurements again and add them together until they arrive at the same figure. This, then, should be the same level as the north end of the tunnel and, slightly lower, is where it must end.

The boy can hardly wait for the digging to start, but Eupalinos is not satisfied with the degree of accuracy of this method. He has learnt from experience that very small inaccuracies can develop into astonishingly large errors of measurement when multiplied over a large area, although he is not exactly sure why. He sets the slaves and workmen to start chiselling out the rock at the northern entrance, but the problem of accuracy of measurement keeps him awake at nights.

The tunnellers use hammers and chisels to dig into the hillside. It is skilled work, and slow. The number working at any one time is restricted by the space available at the work face, which becomes even more confined as the tunnel progresses. Labourers work non-stop to clear the rubble and cart it away.

To keep to the alignment established above-ground, the tunnellers must keep the direction constant, by making sure they keep the ever-diminishing square of light at the entrance directly behind their backs, and in line with a marker placed back at Ayanni, on the opposite side of the ravine. The further they dig into the mountain, the darker it gets, and the poorer the air quality becomes. Clay lamps burn oil to give some light, which only makes the air even more difficult to breath. Men cannot work for too long in these conditions, so the teams of tunnellers are constantly changed, and they, too, work around the clock, so that the work never stops.

Nevertheless, they make slow progress. Eupalinos has calculated the approximate length of the tunnel, and he can now begin to calculate the rate at which his men can work. Even supposing they continue to work at the same rate, which presupposes that there are no unexpected hold-ups – an unlikely scenario – he calculates that at this rate, the tunnel could easily take as much as fifteen years to build. This will not do, he knows. The tyrant will not stand for this. There will be terrible trouble; he will be accused of incompetence or of malingering. He may even be accused of corruption, or deliberate sabotage, or maybe of collaboration with any of the tyrant's many enemies.

He must think of some way to speed up the whole process. Taking Amoun by the shoulder, they climb up to the top of the mountain, up to where the wind ripples in the grass, and they can look down to the city far below. Up here is where he first felt the Gods had encouraged him to take the project on. They stand in silence, the sun beating down on their bare heads, and the wind soughs in the trees like the sound of water rushing down a river bed.

*

VIII

LEVELS AND LEAKAGES

POLYCRATES IS ANGRY. HE wants regular information on what is going on over the mountain, and does not expect to have to send for it. He needs to know exactly how the work is progressing, but that damned engineer hardly ever comes to court. Why not?

"Let him be summoned," shouts the tyrant, "he must learn better manners, and be made to give regular reports." He aims a kick at his Steward, who hurries off to try and see what can be done about this unexpectedly reluctant employee.

On top of the mountain again, the Engineer and his boy are tired and hot. After a while, Eupalinos sighs and sits down to rest under a tree. Amoun squats to play on the ground. He has found an ant's nest, and he pushes a twig into the centre of the little mound, to annoy the ants. The twig is too short, so he finds another one and delicately pushes it in from the other side, so that they meet in the middle. He looks up at his master, and smiles.

His master laughs back at him, and shakes his head. Then thinks again. No, no, not two tunnels, to meet in the middle of the mountain! The idea is not a new one, he tells the boy, but no one has ever dared to attempt it, as it is quite impossible. How could one possibly make the measurements required to ensure that the two tunnels ever meet? We are like moles tunnelling in the dark, he laughs; under the mountain, we are blind.

And yet, he dreams, staring out towards the sea, and his thoughts come to him gently, but surely, like swelling waves towards the sandy beach. If only it could be done... both tunnels could be cut at the same time, and the completion time would be halved! Could it be possible? Eupalinos gazes around him, and his eyes light on the glittering white marble columns of the Heraion temple being constructed on the sea-shore, far away below them, in the distance to the west. He would need more than ordinary help for this. Whom better to beg for help than the great goddess Hera herself, and where better to ask for it than from the architects of her own temple?

*

Theodoros is the younger of the two temple architects and a great favourite of the tyrant. Interested in all things to do with building, he has taken to walking over the mountain to see how the work is going and to share his ideas with Eupalinos. Theodoros is the inventor of a number of architectural and surveying tools, including a useful version of the carpenter's square for measuring right angles. He also brings with him his latest invention: an accurate levelling instrument using water enclosed in a rectangular clay gutter. This is much more convenient to use than the large, unwieldy *chorobates*, a heavy, wooden water level six meters long, mounted on a table, which engineers had used up until now, and it is also a great deal more accurate, as it does not depend only on the human eye. Together, the two of them, engineer and architect, are constantly to be seen around the site now, heads down, deep in discussion.

Theodoros is intrigued by the notion of a double-ended tunnel. And it is just the kind of daring project, he says, never having been done before, which the tyrant will approve. But Eupalinos is agonizingly aware of the infinitely greater degree of accuracy required. A single tunnel need only be roughly horizontal, and can always be modified by degrees to achieve a satisfactory flow of water, whereas two tunnels might miss each other entirely, if the original measurements were not correct.

Eupalinos needs to find a way of double-checking his measurements. Theodoros is interested to try out his new levelling system on a large scale. He suggests they mark a horizontal path the long way round the western side of the mountain, from the tunnel entrance in the north, round towards the spot marked as the southern end, keeping to a constant elevation on the contour by means of his invention. It will take a long time, certainly, but the tunnelling work can continue meanwhile, so nothing will be lost.

So potters are put to work making hundreds of rectangular clay gutters, and stonemasons cut limestone slabs. A series of layered limestone pillars are set up on the path along the way, each one capped by a levelling gutter filled with water. The clay gutters are joined at right angles wherever sighting makes it necessary.

Gradually, they work their way around the mountain-side, joining each piece of guttering to the next, the slaves pouring water in as they go, while Eupalinos insists on checking every level himself. It is an agonizingly slow job, taking months, and many slaves to carry the materials, but when at last they reach the site of the southern end of the tunnel, they find that, indeed, the original marker was inaccurate by the length of several cubits. Now they are able to adjust the marker to reach a degree of accuracy of which even Eupalinos is satisfied, for the smooth, level water in the gutters cannot lie. Theodoros stands back and smiles as the boy dances about, and Eupalinos, his arms raised, calls out his thanks to the Gods.

When next Meandrius the Steward arrives, puffing up the mountain-side, the Engineer is able to give him a satisfyingly encouraging report.

*

Spies, there are spies everywhere, everyone knows that. The tunnel project, and especially its whereabouts, must be kept secret at all costs. The tyrant has a rumour put around that he is mining for silver, and that he has been told by an oracle that a great treasure lies hidden under the mountain. A strong guard is set around the area of the north entrance, and the route of the channel leading to it. So it is, that the workers' camp is to a great extent cut off from the city.

Certain privileged persons are allowed in and out, in particular, Maeandrius who is Polycrates' steward. He it is who has been ordered to make regular inspections as to the progress being made. He is an obsequious yet self-important man, small and nervous. He enjoys displaying the reflected powers of his master the tyrant and shows these off whenever he can. He tells Eupalinos that he must attend at the palace more often, that Polycrates expects that sort of attention. Failure to do so is dangerous; there are many courtiers jealous of this project, who would like to see him fail.

But Eupalinos cannot bear the sycophantic atmosphere of the court, and will leave his post as seldom as possible. A house has been provided for them in the city, but he prefers the atmosphere of the camp, sharing the life with the labourers, content with receiving the Steward on his visits, and totally immersed in his work the rest of the time.

The courtiers are irritated by this odd couple, unsociable and self-contained, Eupalinos so awkward and solitary, and the untamed, elfin boy. No-one can understand why they nevertheless appear to be in favour with the tyrant, judging by the limitless amount of money and materials it is rumoured are being made available for the 'mining' project. Maeandrius will not say a word out of place, but friends of the poet Anacreon have reported back that it certainly cannot be for the Engineer's good looks that he has been chosen, which causes some laughter at court. The boy, however, is a different matter, they say.

And Amoun is inquisitive. For some time now he has taken to wandering off when he is not needed, exploring the island, sometimes down to the sea-shore, sometimes as far as the site of Hera's great temple. His master considers this natural, now that he is growing older.

Running down the southern mountain-side one evening, slashing at poppy heads with his stick, Amoun talks and sings to himself as he goes, kicking dusty, white stones on the path as it winds down the hillside. Goats browse the coarse brown grass, and he stops to chase them for a while then, laughing, walks on down towards the city outskirts.

Suddenly, he is seized from behind. His arms are held tightly, and he feels hot breath on his cheek as a rough voice tells him to be quiet, and not cause trouble. Then he is thrown over a man's shoulder and carried into the main street, to where a group of well-dressed young men stand around, gossiping.

"Is this the one you wanted?" says the slave, grinning, and one of the men tosses him a coin as the boy is set down in front of them. Furious, Amoun immediately runs for his captor, scratching and biting as hard as he can, as the young men roar with laughter. He is taken into a room where more men, and boys, are drinking wine, and he is made to sit down and given a cup of wine himself. He is grubby and dishevelled, red-faced and fierce with anger, and he spits the wine at the other boys, which causes more laughter. He knows what they want him for.

Then a tall and graceful man comes over to Amoun and pulls him to his feet. In a voice of authority, he tells the others:

"I'll take him. This boy is spoken for." There is some grumbling, but this man is too well thought-of at court, for him to be argued with.

It is not until they are outside again that Amoun realises, through the smudge of his tears, that the man is Theodoros. Holding the lad hard by the shoulder, they turn, not into the city, but back up the mountain path. All the way back to the camp, Theodoros is serious and silent. He is afraid that Eupalinos' lack of court manners, and his obvious disdain for the subservient pandering expected from favourites, will sooner or later get him into serious trouble. At the camp gates, he pushes the lad inside, then calls him back.

"Two things, boy", he says, almost fiercely. "Stay closer to your master in future, and tell him to be careful".

Amoun watches him stride away, back to the city where the noise of music and laughter can faintly be heard. It is dark, now, on the mountain-side. He shivers, and rubs the bruise on his shoulder. A wind has lifted, rattling the branches in the trees around him. These are trees he knows well, his everyday companions whom he loves. As the sky darkens, stars appear, and the boy softly whistles through his teeth till the wind, sighing, dies down and there is silence.

Stretching, he gets up and goes in towards the camp-fire where he finds his master already sleeping, wrapped up in his blanket. The boy curls up at his master's feet, where he knows he is safe, wraps his short cloak around his head, and tries to sleep, but is troubled by dark, chaotic dreams. His nightmares are a chaos of terrible fires and forests burning, of boiling rivers and falling rocks. The sky burns darkly, wild and ancient gods hurl thunderbolts and people laugh at him in his terror. He whimpers in his sleep, and his master reaches out and pulls him close, for comfort.

*

Work can start immediately on tunnelling in from the southern end. So the work force is doubled, and the work proceeds at twice the pace. There are no problems: sighting lines back to the new entrance at the south are established in the same way as at the north end, and from there the tunnel proceeds upwards at a gentle gradient.

At the north end, however, things are not going so well. The rock here is porous, becoming much softer than at first, with rivulets of water constantly seeping from the roof and the walls. If the gradient at this end continues to head downwards as planned, the water will collect at the work-face and, as there is no way to drain it, progress will eventually become impossible. Therefore the gradient must, temporarily, be made to rise smoothly upwards until the Engineer estimates the seam of water will be passed. The floor can then return to its original level, and the labourers will be able to work without having to stand knee-deep in water.

*

It may be that Poseidon, Earth-shaker, is angry. Maybe the composition of the rock at the north end is just not suitable for tunnelling. Perhaps the Engineer has not allowed for sufficient roof timbering, or maybe the calamity is caused by a combination of all these things. Whatever the cause, in the dead of night there is suddenly a great cracking sound. With a noise like thunder, rock crashes on rock, tumbles and falls, filling the space with flying stones and boulders. A third of the way into the northern side of the mountain, the roof has caved in.

Eupalinos, lying wrapped in his blanket at the tunnel mouth, is startled from sleep. All around him is screaming and shouting, as men run to light torches, fetch shovels, coughing in the dust which pours from the tunnel mouth. A part of the tunnel roof has fallen, all progress is blocked and eight men are crushed to death under the rocks.

When the calamity at the tunnel is reported, the tyrant, loudly losing his temper, refuses to allow the work to stop for a moment. Is the man he has hired nothing but an incompetent? The Engineer must find another route, he shouts, and quickly, where the rock is more suitable. Eupalinos' enemies at court are delighted to find that he is not, after all, infallible. Now, perhaps, he will have to come at last to court like everyone else, and make himself agreeable.

*

Eupalinos has had experience before of loose rock in a tunnel roof. He remembers a similar problem back in Megara, when he was working with his father and, not for the first time, he longs to be able to consult Naustrophon, if only he could. No matter how quickly the project needs to be completed, the older man never allowed the work to be rushed. He reminds himself of his father's sound advice at the time, and knows that, here, he must take no chances.

First, more labourers must be brought in, to clear away the fallen rock, and, at the same time, to shore up other potentially dangerous parts, in long sections of the tunnel, right back to within 100m of the entrance.

Huge rectangular blocks of stone are cut and dressed outside, then dragged in on wooden rollers, to line the walls. Many of these stone slabs weigh over a ton yet, incredibly, they are hoisted up using ropes and pulleys, and fitted into the tunnel roof to end in a beautiful, pointed arch many metres long. Then, for good measure, the Engineer has the same thing done at the start of the south end. A great deal of time and a great many extra men are required for this skilled work of stone cutting, dressing and fitting of the slabs, but the cutting from the southern end continues as before.

Theodoros the architect comes over from his work in the Temple, to see what is going on under the mountain. He smiles when he sees the simple beauty of the design, and he asks Amoun, gently, why his master has taken such care, inside a tunnel where it will hardly ever be seen? The boy blushes, and says he cannot tell, but he is sure that this is the way it should be done. Would the architect like to see what his master is working on now? Together they make their way deep into the mountain, to where work has resumed at the rock face. Here, Theodoros is astonished to see that the direction of the tunnel has been made to veer towards the west. Eupalinos is there, marking figures on the wall in red paint.

"This rock becomes weaker towards the north-east," he explains to his friend, "so we must dig westwards in order to reach more solid rock. Now that we are no longer digging in a straight line, we cannot see the entrance, to check on our direction. I have calculated that we must continue the digging, at the same level, along one side of a triangle, until I can ascertain that the rock is sufficiently strong.

"Then we can turn back south-east again. If we proceed first south-westwards, then south-eastwards, according to the triangle on the plan you see here, we will eventually arrive back at the same line of direction at which we started, and can then go south again. And I can only calculate this, if I mark the measurements as we go, and then mark them in reverse order until I am satisfied that we have arrived at exactly our original straight course again".

Theodoros is impressed, but wary. He has not studied the mathematics of Thales at Miletus as Eupalinos has, and is less sure of the useful application of triangles for measurement. He protests that there is absolutely no way this can be double-checked. The southern tunnel, meanwhile, is continuing on the same straight line, and what if the two of them were no longer on the same plane? But Eupalinos marks out his triangles and arcs, and explains the geometrical construction to his friend, in the flickering light of the oil lamp, until he is convinced.

Theodoros whistles quietly to himself as he and Amoun walk back down to the tunnel mouth. Such astonishing confidence is dangerous, but thrilling. He offers up a little prayer to Hera, for his friend's sake.

*

All this is faithfully reported back to the tyrant by Maeandrius the steward, but Polycrates, surrounded by sycophants, narrows his eyes, and worries only how soon the Egyptian spies he has bribed will find out the truth.

He has paid them a large amount of silver to report to him secretly on Amasis' covert dealings with the Persians. He knows that this will soon be reported back to the Persians themselves, but how long will it be before the Egyptian spies find out that he has paid even more to the Persians? Or not the Persians, exactly, but their satraps – 'guardians of the King's power' – men like Oreotes, governor of Sardis since it had been taken and Croesus enslaved. For the Persians find it is a simple thing to recruit local strongmen among the Lydian Greeks, willing to accept subjugation at their hands in return for positions of power over their own countrymen.

Polycrates is not afraid of the Egyptians, but he would not like the Persians to know the extent of his dealings with their own satraps. He would not like anyone to know the secret dream of his ambition, which has been growing increasingly pressing over the years: that, on the basis of his increasing dominion over the sea and his careful manipulation of the satrap-governors, he might one day make himself master of all Ionia and the islands.

Polycrates, who thrives on a political situation as volatile as this, likes to feel that he can use men like Oreotes. At the same time, it is precisely men of this type on his own island, of whom he must be most wary. He sends for his steward, Maeandrius, to check again on a list of names he has been secretly compiling for some time now. He has plans for these, the disgruntled aristocrats and landowners who are always there in the back of his mind, false sycophants, hovering at the edges of his dreams, plotting and scheming against him.

For the moment, Eupalinos need not fear any interference with his design for the detour at the northern end of his tunnel.

*

IX

ELENI MAKES A DISCOVERY

M Y DUTIES AT THE Governor's house were not really
very onerous. My position as 'companion' lay somewhere
between that of a servant and a guest, but I was not unkindly
treated. I was grateful to my relatives for having taken me in,
and for the consideration they showed me. My difficulties lay,
not with the heaviness of my duties, but with their unremitting
tedium.

The Governor's wife required me to hold her skein of wool
while it was wound into a ball, or to fetch her various little
things she might need, and sometimes to read to her during
the evenings, during which time she mostly fell asleep. The
Governor was a busy man and often absent from home, and
these evenings seemed very long to me. I longed to find a topic
of conversation which might interest the elderly lady, but I
could not tell myself with any great conviction that I had yet
succeeded.

Monsieur Guerin's arrival had aroused the curiosity of the
whole household and injected a liveliness into it which had not

been there before so that, when he was at home, our evenings no longer dragged. On the occasions when he was away, travelling around the island, or working in his own room, I would find myself talking about my tutor's researches and taking it upon myself to explain and elaborate upon them. I was aware that I sometimes became almost carried away, as though all this new-found knowledge and wisdom were my own. It is in my nature to have a tendency to exaggerate anything which makes me happy.

That evening, I sat at the table in my room and looked critically at myself in the looking glass. This was not something I often did, as I am well aware that I am no beauty. Nevertheless, I could see that my complexion was brighter as a result of all the exercise I had been taking, walking over the terrain with Victor. Taking off my spectacles, I thought my eyes even seemed to be brighter, too. In fact, I decided, my life in the house at Chora had altogether improved as a result of my involvement in my tutor's archaeological investigations.

I did find the older gentleman a pleasant, although often irritating companion, and I most certainly enjoyed acquiring a better knowledge of my island's past. I was constantly impressed by his learning but, oh dear! if only he were not so dreadfully pleased with himself. I had been putting together a collection of drawings I had made of the places we had visited, which I planned to present to him as a gift of thanks. I thought I understood that he did value the contributions I made. To feel valued was something I have not been much accustomed to and so this pleased me immensely.

*

Originally, the outing had been planned merely as a reconnaissance trip, but it had turned out to be much, much more exciting than that.

"As all other attempts to locate this tunnel had so far proved fruitless, we bent our steps towards the chapel of St John (Ayanni)" wrote Monsieur Guérin in his notebook. "Situated to the north of Mt Kastro, half a league from the village of Chora, the chapel is surrounded by seven or eight tumbled down cottages, and a few trees which give a pleasant shade. At its head, the spring gushes out of the earth and collects in a sort of natural basin; thence it overflows, runs over a little wall, and falls in a cascade down into the creek bed.

"Fifteen paces to the right is the chapel of St John. I was informed that it had been built over a vast cistern and, indeed, I could see that water was running out through a number of holes cut into the side walls. Inside the chapel, Commander Alexis dug out one of the paving stones in the floor, and I could see that this 'cistern' was, in fact, a very beautiful ancient reservoir. It was full of water, as it still communicates with the spring by a pipe, which has never been blocked up. It is 2m 30cm deep. Square pillars, made of magnificent rectangular blocks of marble, divide it into three parallel compartments.

"This 'copious spring' (Herodotus' words), the antique reservoir and their position behind Mt Kastro, are favourable indications, I believe, that we had found what we were looking for, and this presumption was made all the more certain when, outside the chapel, looking in a southerly direction, I spied a large groove, 35 cm wide, cut into the rock, which disappeared under a shed, then re-appeared a little further on, then faded out completely as the land climbed towards the mountain. There, beneath the soil, I was amazed to see large blocks of stone, and they were carved into the shape of a vault."

Victor Guérin mopped his face, and put down his notebook. He though again, hard, about what they had discovered. In fact, although he hated to admit it, it had been Eleni who had seen the groove first but, surely, in a discovery as important as this one, some poet's license was allowed him? He looked across to where she was resting under the shade of a tree. How charming she looked, he thought tenderly, her long skirts tucked under her, her large straw hat in her lap. He wished he had the courage to express to her something of what he felt. Not normally a man afflicted with self-doubt, he nevertheless had to admit to himself that this young woman made him feel nervous. There was something about her enthusiasm, her determination and her energy which, though charming in itself, of course, somehow forbade any kind of direct approach.

I wondered what Monsieur was writing in his notebook. I had taken off my spectacles, and was dozing in the heat, re-living the moment when I had seen the groove in the rock, and immediately understood that these very stones were something from ages past. More than two thousand years past, and all that time farmers had farmed around them, donkeys and goats had grazed over them, people had wandered around them, built sheds and cottages by them, but had never noticed them. It was like a miracle! With pleasure, I realised that it was the same as with my drawing: one rarely sees something unless one is actually looking for it.

Carefully placing my fingers on the grooved rock, I had traced it across the field and past the shed, then on to where it plunged underground. Throwing myself on my knees, I had started to scrape away the soil with my bare hands, until M. Guérin hurried towards me, gently chiding as he pulled me to my feet.

"*Non, non, ma petite*. Not like this: we will come back with proper tools and excavate properly, scientifically, my dear, dear Eleni". His hands were warm on the bare skin of my arm, but I turned away, laughing with excitement, to pick up my hat from where it lay on the ground.

Returning to Chora, we were both silent, thinking of the marvel of what we had found. The driver of the pony trap flicked his whip at the pony's head as we trundled back over the bumpy, uneven stones laid along the road. The trap clattered along, swaying from side to side so that I am afraid we could not help, as we went along, that our knees continually touched, then separated, then touched again. It was quite embarrassing, but could not be avoided.

*

To his increasing alarm, however, Victor began to find this touching almost unbearably erotic. Worse still, as the vehicle turned sharply into the gate, Eleni was thrown off balance, and had to lean heavily on his arm before righting herself, with a murmured apology. At the door, he made sure to help her down gallantly, and she looked up into his face, and smiled her thanks.

The Governor's wife, looking out of the window as they approached, saw it all, and became thoughtful. She knew nothing about Monsieur Guerin, other than that he had been recommended to her husband by an acquaintance at the French consulate in Athens. She would be rather sorry to lose her companion, she thought but, if this might be a chance for the poor young woman, it would make no sense to stand in her way. And so it came about that no difficulties were made about the amount of time Eleni was able to spend alone with the foreign gentleman.

*

The Commander's convicts were not available immediately, so Victor and I spent the intervening days wandering over the southern side of the mountain, to see if we could find the place where the tunnel could be expected to come out. Much of the mountain higher up was covered with scrub and, lower down, with olive trees, so our search took us over dry, stony pastures grazed by scrawny goats, over tumbled-down walls and ruined stone huts and cottages.

Ragged children stared at us as we passed; at other times we wandered into dark enclosures where the floor was covered with goat droppings, and we would be startled by the sudden, high bleating of a kid, tied to a post by a leather strip. We were searching for some sign of a water conduit, or a fountain, but we found nothing. It was difficult to determine the limits of the old city.

"Herodotus clearly tells us that the water was led from the tunnel right into the city" insisted M. Guérin. "Yet how can we tell where this might be, when these wretches have stolen all the stones of the ancient walls?"

Waving his arms irritably, he marched off across the dusty fields towards what might once have been a fountainhead, or perhaps just another heap of stones piled up by the farmer when he cleared his land. There had been several such puzzling piles of limestone blocks, but none of them, on examination, seemed at all like an ancient fountain. I caught up with him as he sat down, exhausted, in the shade of the stones to take a drink from his water bottle. I, too, was tired and dusty, and the heel of my button boot had come loose, making walking difficult.

The sun beat down; it was terribly hot. After a little while I noticed that my companion had fallen asleep. I breathed a small sigh of relief, I have to say, as my tutor was being so very irritable that day. I took out my sketchbook, and began to draw the stem of grass by my foot. I believe I am a woman who can find beauty in many things, and I have had had plenty of practice at making the best of a situation.

I was absorbed in my drawing. I loved the way the dry seed head of the grass contained so many tiny flowerets; on my paper, they appeared as complex and as lovely as a hothouse flower. After a while I realised that my tutor had woken and was talking to me, but I am afraid I did not pay much attention, concentrating on my work. It seemed that Victor was struggling to express his thoughts.

"A man of science, like myself, is necessarily a solitary person, fated to pursue his life's work to the exclusion of a life of domesticity." he said. "I have travelled in many countries, and have had the great good fortune to have achieved some small renown in my chosen field of study, though I do say it myself. I have found much happiness in the pursuit of knowledge."

I confess I was really becoming rather tired of his constant references to his own intelligence. At that moment, I was much more interested in the sharp, straight edge of the dry blade of my grass, in contrast to its delicately drooping head; such a lovely juxtaposition.

M. Guérin continued: "When such a person finds, or feels that he may have found, another person who seems to share his passion for knowledge, and of history, and who appears to be willing to accompany him in this pursuit, then this is an important thing, no? I hope you understand that I am sometimes driven almost crazy by the *bétise*, the stupidity, of people who do not care about history, not even when it is their own."

At this, I put aside my drawing (it was almost finished, anyway), and turned to listen more closely. Thinking back, I am now not sure, but I think he may have been about to place his hand on mine! He gave a little cough.

"So you are not disgusted, when I expostulate, sometimes maybe a little strongly, about them? I think I may have seen you smile, sometimes, when I shout aloud my feelings".

Appalled at the thought that I might have offended the poor old gentleman, I assured him as fulsomely as I could, that I was not disgusted at all. I respected, on the contrary, his passion for ancient things. I enjoyed our excursions immensely, I told him.

On our way home in the governor's pony trap, I thought M. Guérin mumbled something about not having made himself quite clear. I decided to change the subject. I was pleased with my drawing and therefore with my day, so I determined to be cheerful and animated.

"As all this seaward side of the mountain appears to be so very dry", I said, "It seems that the tunnel, wherever it may be, is certainly no longer functioning, nor has been for some considerable time. I do wonder what happened to it in the end, and why it became lost, and when that was?"

Victor Guérin sighed. I hoped that he had understood that his previous topic of conversation was not to be resumed. I knew that he was always pleased to discuss a historical subject, however and indeed, after a short pause, he replied enthusiastically:

"The building of the overland aqueduct by the Romans, about one thousand years later, indicates that by then the supply of water was no longer considered sufficient. However, it does not necessarily mean that the tunnel was replaced; both might have continued in use together for a while. There is some record, I believe, of the tunnel being used as a hiding place from pirates, as late as the 7th century anno domini, which would seem to suggest that it was still there, but that water no longer flowed through it by then."

At the governor's residence I was feeling dusty and hot, so chose to retire at once. My tutor bowed as I left the room. He would have kissed my hand before I went, but I withdrew it very firmly, so that he did not dare.

Looking out of the window in my little room, I realised that I was going to have to be more careful. I most certainly did not wish to offend, and I dearly wanted to continue our lessons, so I became somewhat apprehensive.

Victor Guerin's notes for that day, when he came to write them up, were brief: "A disappointing day. I did not manage to discover any of the things I was hoping to find."

*

X

Difficulties and Danger

About 525 BC

As the years pass, the tunnel continues to penetrate deep into the mountain from both ends. For some time now there have been no major disasters in the construction of this massive undertaking, although there is always, of course, a certain cost in the lives or injuries of the labouring slaves.

Amoun is now no longer a child, but a young man, and Eupalinos' beard is showing signs of grey. Polycrates' daughter, Parthenope, naturally, has also grown, and changed. She is not yet often seen in public.

Walking down the central street, on a rare visit to the city to fetch some stores for his master, Amoun happens to pass the temple of Aphrodite, where a small crowd is gathered. The women from the palace, Parthenope among them, are making an offering of honey cakes to the Goddess, whose statue stands at the entrance. He stares in surprise at the striking young girl she has become.

Surrounded by her maids, she walks proudly down the steps, affecting not to notice the interest she evokes around her. Amoun smiles at her as she passes, but she is haughty and turns her back on him. Now fourteen years old, and of an age to be married, she has grown unexpectedly beautiful and is renowned, it is said, for her cleverness as well as for her sharp tongue and her bad temper.

*

Eupalinos hates to leave the tunnel site for any length of time but, nevertheless, on a number of occasions, he has felt obliged to present himself at the palace, trying to make himself agreeable, but without much success, being neither sociable nor talkative by nature. His only real interest at the moment is the progress of work on the tunnel, of which he will not speak.

Sometimes, very reluctantly, he takes the lad with him. Now Parthenope sits beside her father, and Amoun cannot take his eyes off her. Her beauty is glittering, intoxicating it seems to him. He is dazzled by her, by her long white arms, her pale skin and deep black eyes. She ignores him completely and yet, he thinks it is as though, without even turning, she has let loose an arrow and wounded him to the death. He understands that he is a prisoner, spell bound, and wonders how he can have allowed this to happen to him.

Most of the courtiers appear to have lost all interest in the so-called 'mining project' up on the mountain, which does not seem to have produced much silver yet, and Eupalinos receives at most a curt nod of the head from the tyrant whenever he presents himself. Polycrates' court is a place of fear for them all, where both rewards and punishments are always excessive, and always arbitrary. No one is safe from the tyrant's displeasure, and the cruelty of his anger.

And Polycrates is extremely displeased to hear that Pythagoras, the trouble-maker, has returned from Egypt. Epaulinos knows that Amoun has visited the Sage since his return hoping, perhaps, to hear him talk in the language of animals, or explain to him more fully how all things are connected, one to another. Back at the camp, the Engineer questions the lad about Pythagoras' great knowledge of mathematics and especially of the power of triangles, but Amoun shrugs.

"He says that it is Order" he replies, "which is the regulating principle of the whole universe, but you already know this, Master, for the universe is governed by mathematical relations, as you yourself have taught me. This Sage is wonderfully clever but, as far as I can tell, it may be that he is interested more in abstractions than in applications."

His master tells the lad not to visit again, as the tyrant has put a watch on the man and Eupalinos fears there could be trouble. Reluctantly, Amoun agrees, foreseeing that Pythagoras will not stay in Samos for long.

And indeed, the Sage is ordered into exile again, after declaring to his followers that the tyranny of Polycrates is a despotic regime too oppressive for a free man to endure. He is ordered to leave for Italy, where he establishes a school at Croton and it is here that he grows famous. So famous, in fact, that after his death there are some of his followers who even believe him to been a god in human form.

*

Samos has continued to flourish and prosper under Polycrates. The city walls are complete, as is the harbour. Fine, well-built stone houses and shops have been constructed along both sides of the main street, which is well-paved, allowing the townspeople a pleasant space in which to promenade on warm summer evenings.

The tyrant observes with satisfaction his fleet of ships, his thousand archers and other military precautions and, at least for now, ignores the slow progress of the tunnel. For the moment, the island is quiet; many of the principle agitators have left of their own accord and Polycrates' complex system of political checks and balances appears to be holding firm.

Cyrus the Great, King of Persia, is dead, killed in battle far away to the east, beyond even Babylon and Assyria, in a land known as the country of the Massegetae. After the battle the Queen and General of their army had ordered a search to be made for Cyrus' body. Severing the head, she flung it into a skin filled with human blood, so that the Great King would, at last, have his fill of blood.

But then comes news that his son, Cambyses, has succeeded him, a man of whom it is rumoured that he is at least half mad. Spectacular stories of impiety, excess and ferocious cruelty are listened to with horror, as the old fear is resurrected and it is whispered that Cambyses intends to turn his Persians once more towards the West. Cambyses has married his own sisters, and then killed them in a fit of rage. He has murdered his brother. He has used his cup-bearer for target practice, and shot him dead. Courtiers whose advice he dislikes are buried alive, head downwards, or their sons are slaughtered.

Polycrates does not hesitate. He sends a message of the utmost politeness to the Persian ambassador.

*

Eupalinos may be a self-sufficient man, withdrawn from the world around him and uninterested in the necessaries of civilization outside his own focus. Nevertheless, he finds he depends more and more heavily upon Amoun, for help and for company, as they grow older. He knows the young man is quick and eager to learn, always original in his thinking and prescient in foreseeing what needs to be done. Recently, though, he seems absent minded and lacking in concentration, and his master worries about him.

No longer able to seek knowledge from Pythagoras the sage, Amoun has taken to spending all his spare time hanging around the town, not daring to enter the palace by himself, yet hoping to catch sight of Parthenope if by chance she should show herself. And sometimes he is lucky: she likes sometimes to parade herself in the town, always surrounded by her ladies, superbly dressed and pampered, enjoying the stir she makes as she passes. She has noticed the beautiful young man who stares at her so longingly, and she smiles in satisfaction at his discomfiture. She makes sure he has seen that she is aware of his presence, but disdains to acknowledge it. She is far too highly-born to allow a mere commoner to approach her.

Amoun cannot sleep. At night he leaves the snores and grunts of the other men behind, and makes his way into the thick forest to the north, where the old trees creak and mutter as he passes. He crosses the spring with its water swiftly running, until he reaches a clearing where a single, ancient oak stands by itself. He needs a place where he can pray to the gods, alone, where he can beg to be freed from the spell which he believes has bound him to Parthenope.

He prays to Aphrodite, Goddess of love, as he must. He begs for mercy but she is playful, arbitrary and whimsical in her responses; his mind races and he stumbles in his prayers. Feeling out of his depth he tries again, and opens his heart instead to Artemis, the huntress, lover of the sacred forests. The power of her magic is to hunt down the desires of the heart, and always to obtain them. She is the essence of pursuit. She will better understand him, he thinks, that his desire is not for conquest, but for release. The Goddess sends no sign, yet, that she has heard him.

The love-sick youth wanders wistfully back to the camp, stopping by the way to converse with the dryads of the trees and the water nymphs, as he used to do years ago when he first arrived in Samos. He feels cheered by the familiar sighing of the trees and the chuckle of flowing water in the stream, and takes this for a good omen. He arrives back at the camp as dawn is breaking, where he finds his master is waiting anxiously for him. The young man's mood sinks again, thinking of the darkness inside the tunnel, the thick air, the overpowering stench of sweat and shit, the smell of the dark. He feels suddenly faint; he fears that he is ill, he tells his master, he cannot work today.

The Engineer is shocked. He cannot afford to let his assistant fall sick; he needs him by his side, for his encouragement and his questions, and for the lad's help in the constant work of translating the sometimes impenetrable workings of the Engineer's mind into practical instructions for the labourers. "Go and sleep," he tells Amoun "tomorrow you will feel better" and strides away towards the tunnel mouth, his mind already on the coming day's problems.

For never has Eupalinos attempted a task so difficult, nor one so dangerous. Many more of the workmen and slaves have been injured or died, crushed under falling rock or asphyxiated in the almost airless conditions, or simply collapsed from exhaustion. At the northern end of the tunnel, where much of the rock is fragile, there have been constant smaller falls. More huge stones have had to be quarried and cut to shore up the roof, and to line both tunnel entrances. Plasterers have made waterproof cement to seal these up and keep out the dripping water.

Eupalinos has grown used to thinking of Amoun almost as an extension of himself; he is surprised at the young man's sudden show of weakness, and wonders what may have brought this on. The air inside the tunnel is not good, he knows; perhaps this is Amoun's problem?

He will send him for a while to Theodoros, at the site of the Heraion, to learn some of the arts of temple construction. Amoun is a creature of light and air; let him live for a few weeks out there on the seashore where the temple is being constructed, where he can feel the wind and the sun and spend his days in the open. He will return refreshed, ready to take up his tasks again, as his master needs him to be.

At the Temple construction site, all is sunlight and shining white marble; bright light glances off the sea, tossed among the waves and reflected from gleaming columns and great slabs of uncut marble. The site is huge: over 130 great columns are planned, each one the height of more than a dozen men standing upon each other's shoulders. To Amoun the site seems to stretch away forever, so used has he become to working in the confined spaces of his master's tunnel.

There is much for him to learn here. Theodoros shows him his latest invention and Amoun opens his eyes wide in surprise and delight; it is a rotating drill, used to speed up the work of drilling through marble. He is enthralled by the simplicity and efficiency of the design and, under Theodoros's guidance, soon learns to master this new skill. All over the site, craftsmen are working on sculpting the marble into beautiful designs of flowers, acanthus leaves, circles, rosettes or ribbons or palms. Amoun wanders among the shining marble steps and levels, marvelling at so much beauty. As the days go by he feels his heart growing lighter. He decides he can confide in Theodoros.

"Listen, my lad," says Theodoros "listen to the beauty of this place, hear the cries of the gulls, and the crash of the sea spray; feel the presence of mighty Hera, queen of Olympia, wife of Zeus, protectress of Samos. She is the Mother, and She is here in this place and will help us all."

Amoun feels the comforting presence of the Goddess. At night he chooses to sleep in the open air, beside her great altar, and he dreams. He dreams he is sitting high up somewhere in the sunlight, looking down at beautiful Parthenope, scornful and disdaining, and he sees from afar the shadow of his own unrequited and foolish desires. He dreams of his master, alone and troubled, crouching under the weight of the mountain. Will the tunnel ever be finished? And if it is not, will they ever be free to return to the home they left so many years ago? His master needs him, he knows this. He will offer his hopeless love to the Goddess, as a sacrifice. In return, she will grant that the tunnel may be completed with success.

He dreams at last that the Goddess has heard him; he can at last be free of the love-spell which has held him, and he knows, now, what he must do.

*

Back at the tunnel site, Eupalinos is greatly relieved to see him. He has been much missed, by the workmen as well as by his master. Full of the things he has seen and learned and with a light heart, Amoun finds he can now go back inside the darkness without feeling ill; he believes that Hera holds him firmly in her hand, and will not let him fall again.

The day comes when the two of them must visit Polycrates' court again, to deliver another report on their progress.

Theodoros is also there, and welcomes them with a smile. When Parthenope makes her entrance, dazzlingly beautiful, confident of adoration on all sides, Amoun turns away and does not even look at her.

*

For years, now, the Engineer has continually buried himself in a fury of calculations to ensure that they are still on track and keeping to the alignment. He continues to mark these measurements in red paint on the sides of the tunnel. So sure is he of the accuracy of his calculations, that he paints the word *"paradegma"*, 'example to be followed', on the wall to mark where he worked out his first deviation, returning to a straight line to avoid the rock fall. He writes this in case such a necessity should occur again.

At the southern end, the quality of the rock is better, and the work correspondingly faster. Here, Eupalinos has been careful to sink a shaft, stone-lined and dressed, through which light falls into the tunnel. As long as the tunnellers can see both the tunnel mouth and the shaft foot, they are on the right line. Where slight bends are necessary, rock is chopped out from the inside wall, to maintain this line of sight, but the deeper they penetrate, the more difficult it becomes.

If only they could sink more of these shafts as the tunnel progresses! But the further into the hillside that they dig, the higher is the mountain above them, and it quickly becomes far too high above the tunnel to allow for shafts. Eupalinos plods over the mountain and back again several times a day, checking the progress of the two tunnels and his calculations but, for the last few years, he knows that they have been tunnelling absolutely blind.

He has nothing but his own, entirely abstract, calculations to rely on. That, and the favour of the Gods.

*

As the months and years go by, and both tunnel faces continue their infinitely slow advance, blow by blow, chisel cut by chisel cut, weary bucket load by bucket load, Eupalinos feels sure that they must be very close to meeting. He knows the estimated length of the whole tunnel, by adding up the horizontal distances between his original sighting poles over the top of the mountain, and he can measure how far they have dug. But to what extent, if any, might they have deviated from the intended line?

As he has no way of knowing, he opts for the safest strategy, and makes the northern tunnel turn to the west, while the southern tunnel continues in a straight line. He then returns the northern tunnel eastward again, to cross the original alignment at an angle. By doing this, the northern tunnel should cross the southern tunnel as they both advance.

He longs, now, for the tunnel to be completed, so that they can return home to Megara, where his father is waiting for him. He worries that there has been no news from him for months. After all these years, his father will be growing old.

He enters the southern end of the tunnel again, to check, for the hundredth time, that it is still on a straight course. He sees that it is, and yet, something is wrong. Why can he hear nothing from the the expected crossing of the northern heading which, by his calculations, should by now be well within earshot of the sound of pick blows from the other side? Yet there is no sound inside that dark tunnel. Nothing but a thick, heavy silence. Slowly, the awful truth comes to him, that the tunnels do not meet.

The tunnels do not meet! What can have happened? Eupalinos is in a flurry of dread, lest word should get out, and reach the tyrant's ears. He must not let it be known that they are even close to meeting, or he will be subjected to demands for information and questions to which he does not know the answer.

He measures and re-measures, calculates and re-calculates, as the tunnellers continue to chip away, and at last reaches the conclusion that he must have played his hand too soon. He must have underestimated the total length of the tunnel.

The only thing to do now, he thinks, is to continue the northern tunnel forwards, and turn the southern tunnel eastwards, in its turn. Over the next few days Eupalinos, Amoun, the tunnellers and even the basket slaves all watch and wait anxiously as the work proceeds, inch by painful inch. But still the two tunnels do not meet.

He tells the tunnellers to leave him for a while. Content to receive an unaccustomed break, they throw down their tools, their voices fading as they head off towards the entrance to rest. Eupalinos is alone under the mountain, almost at its centre, and he feels the vast weight of it above him. Womb-like, the mountain enfolds him, pressing down and around him as he crouches there, holding his knees pressed to his chest and he, too, prays to Hera, Samos's great protectress. He closes his eyes, rocking slightly, and almost sleeps.

Maybe the Goddess hears him. In the silence at the centre of the great mass of rock, he works again at his numbers, estimating angles and measurements in his head, with all the force of his great intellect, and the strength of all that he has ever learned and experienced in his life as an engineer.

Clearly, he must expand the possible front where the two ends could meet while, at the same time, not waste time and effort by tunnelling more than is necessary. So, in his mind's eye, he turns the direction of the northern end sharply towards the south-west, while turning the southern tunnel north-westwards. Now they must surely cross, he is convinced, for this gives him a much larger possible meeting point, at the earliest possible point where this could be.

It is a brilliant and daring strategy. The labourers are made to redouble their efforts and the work goes forward furiously, but for some time, still, the tunnels do not meet. Yet Eupalinos appears calm and confident now.

*

Maybe the problem is not only one of direction, but of elevation? To make sure, he orders the toiling labourers to increase the vertical section of both tunnels, raising the ceiling of the northern one and lowering the floor of the southern one, so that the possible contact surface is almost four times as large.

He now turns both headings directly towards each other, and offers up a prayer to all the Gods. Amoun refuses to leave the tunnel at all, but lives and sleeps day after day at the southern face, his ear pressed to the rock, listening for the sound of pick-blows from the other side.

The morning comes when the Engineer, tramping up the southern tunnel to the rock-face, finds his shoulder gripped in the dark, and sees, close up, the grin on his boy's dirty face. He is pulled roughly to the rock-face, the tunnellers stand back, and Amoun presses his master's ear to the spot where they have chiselled. Faintly, from the other side, he hears the tap, tap, tap of pick blows.

The two tunnels are not quite in line, but they are not far out. The northern one is too far to the east by about a half a degree. By cutting a final curved hook, they come together, and the tunnellers break through the last slabs of rock with a thundering crash, yelling in triumph as they tumble through. At the actual point of junction, the floor level of the north tunnel is now higher than the south, by about the height of a man's step; a truly minute discrepancy compared to the total distance excavated.

Now, at last, he can announce his success. He has pulled off the most astonishing feat of engineering ever accomplished. Surely, now, his name will resound forever in the ears of men, as '*One who brings things to a successful conclusion*'.

Ah, *Hubris!* The Gods prick up their ears and smile. They love a trick, and their tricks can be cruel. For the project is not yet concluded, and water does not yet run downhill through the tunnel.

*

Accustomed always to getting his way, maybe Polycrates is getting careless as to whom he offends. Over the years the tangle of political relationships and alliances he has woven has been growing ever more complex until, as Herodotus tells us, the noose begins slowly, inexorably, to tighten around him.

Some years before, a ship had arrived at the port, touching in for supplies before going on to the Asian mainland. It had come from Corinth with a cargo on board of three hundred boys, all of them sons of the leading families of Corcyra. Periander, the tyrant of Corinth, was sending them as a gift to the Persian satrap in Sardis, to be made into eunuchs. Corcyra was a vassal state of Corinth, but the two peoples had always been on bad terms, and Periander had chosen these poor boys to make an example of the aristocratic troublemakers.

The Samian courtiers, when they heard of this, had promptly stolen the boys, sending them to take refuge in the temple of Artemis, and refusing to let the Corinthians drag them away. They organised a festival with dancers who carried honey cakes to the boys each day, and there was much laughter at the discomfiture of the Corinthian guards. Eventually the guards were obliged to leave the island without the boys, to the great anger of Periander when he heard of it. Polycrates took no notice when the Corinthian complained; he was always happy to have a plentiful supply of boys at his court.

In this, he has certainly overstepped the mark, for Corinth is a powerful city state. It is especially powerful when in alliance with Sparta, which is now the case, as Periander vows he will avenge this insult, and the Spartans are all too ready to oblige. In secret, they have been meeting to begin negotiations.

Polycrates, meanwhile, is more concerned with Cambyses, the new Persian king. He has not responded to Polycrates' overtures but, according to the spies, he is preparing a force to invade Egypt. Rumours continue concerning Cambyses' madness, and this latest invasion is planned as retribution for an insult he considers he has suffered at Amasis' hands. He had requested or, perhaps, demanded Amasis' daughter in marriage but the Pharaoh, afraid his daughter would be used, not as a wife, but as a concubine, had sent instead the daughter of his enemy, the murdered ex-pharaoh Apries, and pretended that she was his own. Nitetis, 'tall and beautiful' as Herodotus tells us, explained Amasis' trickery as soon as she arrived in Persia, revealing that she was the daughter of the defeated Pharoah. This infuriated Cambyses, who immediately began to prepare his revenge.

Cambyses in Egypt would be rather too close to home for Polycrates. While Cyrus the Great had been busy campaigning far away in the East there had been a breathing space for the Greeks, but Egypt is a different matter, closely tied, as it is, in alliances with many of the Greek city states. Which side would be safer for Polycrates to choose to support? Many of his advisors would prefer to stick with Egypt, but the tyrant is very sure that the Persians, led by mad Cambyses, are by far the most dangerous enemy. Besides, he thinks he sees, in this situation, a way to kill two birds with one stone.

He sends another flattering letter to the Persian king, in which he offers to contribute a naval force to the coming campaign against Egypt. Cambyses graciously accepts the offer. In return, Polycrates begs that the crews of his boats should never be allowed to return to Samos. He then mans forty triremes with carefully selected crews of all the men he suspects of being disloyal to him: disgruntled aristocrats and landowners, relatives of Samians who have been exiled, any man suspected of bearing a grudge, and sends the triremes off to meet Cambyses in Egypt.

XI

SETBACKS

No great celebrations accompany the extraordinary engineering feat of the two tunnels meeting so neatly. Eupalinos receives no resounding triumph, no thank offerings are made to the Gods, no songs composed in his praise. As far as the tyrant is concerned, this is still an unfinished project, of no use to him until the town is satisfactorily supplied with water. He is encouraged in this opinion both by courtiers jealous of the engineer's favoured status, and by the tyrant's military advisers who, perhaps, see the gathering political storms more clearly than does Polycrates himself. Maeandrius the steward comes scuttling over to the camp to urge the Engineer to hurry on with the work, as the summer has again been scorchingly hot and popular sentiment correspondingly irritable at the scarcity of water.

For Eupalinos, however, what remains to be done now is mere hack-work: the feed channel he had marked out from the spring at Ayanni must now be finished and covered over, and the 5,000 lengths of clay pipe which have been manufactured for the purpose must be fitted together and laid along inside the tunnel to carry the water through. A second channel has already been dug, in preparation, from the southern end of the tunnel into the city centre, where Theodoros has been instructed to sculpt four monumental fountains from which the citizens will be able to draw their water in hydrias. No especially difficult problems are envisaged now.

But the geology of Greece is fragile: Poseidon Earth-Shaker is often angry. The island of Samos is no exception and in the years which have passed since Eupalinos made his original measurements, it seems that something disastrous has happened. The land around Ayanni must have shifted slightly, for the water no longer gushes from the spring at quite the same level as before.

It is Amoun who first discovers the calamity. Loyal and loving to his master, he is still considered an odd youth, barely civilised, according to the city folk who may have caught sight of him from a distance. They are fascinated by reports they have heard, telling of his solitary rambles at night, where he is said to talk to trees and rocks. Can it be true, they whisper to each other, that the forest spirits also speak back to him?

Why, he wonders one hot night, as he dips his cup into the cistern for a cool drink, why does it seem that some of the rocks he knows so well, seem to have turned away from him, and why does he have to reach so much further down to fill his cup?

In the early morning, before the camp stirs, he stumbles back to fetch his master, who is making ready to go out across the two river beds which lie between the camp and the spring. What Amoun has divined during long nights of watching, the Engineer is able to verify by careful measurement. The earth and rock have indeed shifted, and it seems that the spring-head has subsided. Not by very much, but enough. The spot where the water emerges is lower, now, than the entrance to the tunnel.

The two stare at each other, as they grasp the meaning of this new problem. If they now follow the original plan for the feed channel, the water will not flow into the tunnel at all.

Yet the spring water will only flow where it can flow; there is nothing to be done about that. Eupalinos stares for a long time at the spring, at the two river beds between it and the mountain, and at the contours of the hillside, while Amoun crouches down and whispers to the Naiads he seems to see in the cool water. Slowly, the Engineer realises that there is only one possible solution, in fact. They will have to deepen the tunnel, all the way, along its entire length.

The tunnel floor being, for the moment, roughly horizontal, to cut a slope into it where the pipes are to be laid had always been part of the original plan, but it had been assumed that this second cutting would start at the same level as the tunnel entrance. Now, to ensure that the water flows downhill all the way, the pipe cutting will have to start before the entrance to the northern end, and at some distance below it. At the southern end where it exits, Eupalinos estimates, it will therefore have to reach right down to a depth of eight and a half metres, a huge job, requiring much more time and much more labour.

Will the tyrant accept this new delay? Well, he will have to accept it, as the Engineer himself has to; there is no other possibility. However, there are several ways in which the work could be speeded up, and Eupalinos makes sure to explain these carefully to Maeandrius, the Steward.

First, it will not be necessary to dig the pipe channel out for its full length, but merely to cut shafts from the tunnel floor down to the required depth every 10 or 12 metres, and then link these together underground. Then again, the labourers can pile up the material they dig out, onto the tunnel floor above: no need to carry it all away. Finally, many more labourers can be set to work all along the length of the tunnel at the same time, so the work will proceed far quicker than before. It might not even take more than one more year to complete the whole project, after which, Eupalinos supposes, he could claim his reward, offer up his thanks to the Gods and return, at last to Megara.

The Steward shakes his head dolefully as Eupalinos explains. To deliver bad news to the tyrant is always dangerous. Fortunately, though, Maeandrius finds, on his return, that his news is swept aside. The whole palace is in uproar and Polycrates in a fury with the spies who have just arrived to report the even worse news they have had from Egypt, concerning Cambyses and the forty triremes full of Samian dissidents.

Polycrates in a fury can be very terrible. The Samian exiles had reached Egypt and had duly been imprisoned by Cambyses. However, they had managed to escape, or maybe they had been allowed to do so – who could tell? They are now on their way back to Samos, say the spies, ready to do battle with their perfidious ruler. And Polycrates knows that many of the families of his exiled subjects on the island so hate him that they are highly likely to join with the exiles against him.

The tyrant strides up and down, shouting for his generals, and cursing mad Cambyses for a traitor and a pact breaker. He will be forced to destroy his own triremes, if it comes to a sea battle. He has his hundred *pentekonters* and his thousand bowmen: how dare these men come against him in this way? Yet he knows that if they have somehow managed to confer with any of the disgruntled landowners on the island, and they rise against him, he will be caught in the middle. In his fear and his fury, he decides on an appallingly cruel strategy. His subjects must be reminded who holds the power on Samos.

Polycrates' soldiers spread out over the whole island, forcing their way into the dwellings of all landowners or potentially suspect subjects, breaking down doors and seizing any who try to resist, although few do. They drag away their wives and children and drive them, screaming and weeping, down to the sea shore, where they shut them up in the boat-sheds. If even *one* man rises up in support of the exiles, thunders the tyrant, the sheds will be set on fire, and all the wives and children burned to death inside them.

The landowners know their tyrant well by now. They know that he will do exactly as he says. Polycrates' move has its desired effect.

The exiles arrive, expecting to find a revolution on the island, and many armed men waiting to join them. Battle is joined at sea, but Polycrates pretends to turn tail and has his ships return to harbour. So the exiles beach their boats, but find to their dismay that no support is forthcoming from anywhere on Samos. Their force, alone, has no chance against Polycrates' paid mercenaries, and they are massacred without pity. Those who can, take the only possible course and turn tail. A number of them do manage to get back to the ships, and these exiles, dispossessed of everything, sail away. With nothing left to lose, they will try their luck and look for help from Sparta.

Graciously, Polycrates thanks his remaining subjects for their loyalty, and returns their families to them. They have learned another harsh lesson, and there is contemptuous laughter, at court. Some months later, the spies report that the exiles have reached Sparta and have been well received.

*

While labourers start immediately on the cutting for pipes inside the tunnel (the exact declination can be fine-tuned later), Eupalinos is concentrating hard on the design of the feed channel, from Ayanni to the northern tunnel mouth. Everything depends on the accurate measurement of levels here, and he cannot risk the slightest problem occurring now.

Where the channel begins, at the spring itself, it can be disguised as a local watering place, but as soon as the level permits, it must go hidden underground, cut into the rock just below the surface. The roof of the channel is vaulted with cope stones, for easier access. Where the rock disappears, the work continues by setting low walls into the ground, covered by horizontal blocks of stone which can then be covered with earth. The channel must wind around the contour, at a constantly declining level, to avoid two ravines, and traverse two small hills between them, before arriving at the foot of Mount Kastro, where the northern entrance is. Where possible, as the depth increases, at certain intervals shafts are dug to give light and let in air to the channel below, and these must be lined with blocks of stone to prevent them collapsing.

When, after some months, the channel begins to approach the tunnel mouth, the cutting inside the tunnel is dug down to a depth which links up with it. The final adjustments can then be made to the floor of this secondary cutting inside the tunnel, to ensure a steady fall: at the southern end, where water will emerge at last, this cutting will be more than twice as deep as at the northern end.

At last, the 5,000 cylindrical sections of clay water pipe, which the potters have been preparing for so long, are carted over the mountain and fitted inside the channel running from Ayanni, then into the second cutting inside the tunnel, keeping a steady fall the whole way. At the southern end, the pipes continue into the final channel leading into the centre of the ancient city. Now, one day very soon, surely, water will flow into the city, and gush from the fountains there, at last?

XII

VICTOR GUERIN
REFLECTS

THERE WAS ANOTHER PLEASANT spot in the courtyard of the villa at Chora, where the old olive tree cast a cooler shade and a garden seat had been placed out of the sun. I often sat there as it was a place no one ever used. I was trying to remember just what had been said the previous day, and I wished I had paid more attention. There had been some sort of clumsy apology for my tutor's irascibility when confronted with what he called the islanders' stupidity, but there had been something more which I thought he had said, something about a life of domesticity?

I could not remember, and could not work it out. Nevertheless, I did feel that perhaps I should show more reserve when engaged on archaeological research with Monsieur Guérin. This new interest in the history of the island was so very precious to me, and I liked to feel that he appreciated me as a useful assistant. It would not do to allow any hint of confusion there. Nevertheless, when it was announced that Commander Alexis and his convicts were ready to start, I felt my spirits rise with the excitement so that, in spite of myself, I joined my tutor in the pony trap with enthusiasm and a bright smile.

I had the impression that Victor had also, meanwhile, decided to be rather more circumspect in his manner, and I felt relieved. He smiled back at me benignly and began to explain the plan of action to me. We would open a number of trenches, following the line of the few metres of supposed tunnel which we had already uncovered together, to see exactly where it led, and then, having established its true direction, the men would begin to excavate more thoroughly.

Like the good scholar that he was, Monsieur Guérin wrote up his notes every night. Would Mademoiselle Eleni be willing, he asked, to go over the notes with him when they were written up, to be sure that nothing had been left out? Of course, I said, I would be more than willing. So it was arranged that we would meet in the evenings after dinner, under the olive tree.

*

Guerin went happily to work, for surely the intimacy of working together in the softness of the evenings, with the sound of the sea in the distance and only the cicadas for company, might lead to a mutual understanding at last? He thought that it must be so, as he started to write up the notes for his publication:

'I must thank Commander Alexis', he wrote, 'who gave me his active and intelligent help and who, for the whole month during which these excavations were carried out, never ceased to support my work with zeal and devotion. Thanks to him, I was given the means to succeed, and I did succeed. Therefore it is my great pleasure to acknowledge his part in the success of the enterprise.

Work was begun at the source of the spring, where an arch had been carved into the rock. This arch continued as a small tunnel, about 80 centimetres wide, filled with gravel and fallen earth and, at the bottom, a considerable number of fragments of thick clay pipe. Surely these must be the pipes mentioned by Herodotus? 'the tunnel...along which water from a copious spring is led by pipes into the town'.

Yet if so, why was this tunnel so small, when Herodotus tells us it was 8 feet wide and 8 feet high? We continued uncovering this tunnel along its length, rather than its depth, so that we might arrive more quickly at a larger part. One week later, we had advanced about 24 paces. His Honour the Governor was so kind, at this point, as to take the time to visit our excavations and, after him, the entire population of Chora came rushing to have a look. We continued amidst this general excitement, filled with the hope that we might succeed in restoring to the island, at least in part, one at least of the marvels of its former glory.

However, at the end of this our first trench, considerable rock falls, including some enormous stones, made it impossible to continue on that line.

The hillside went on upwards and 15 paces further on we came across a ravine. The tunnel seemed to have been washed away completely here, so there was no purpose in excavating further. We hope, nevertheless, to be able to make a third opening further up the mountain.'

After dinner, with an air of ceremony, Monsieur Guerin handed me this finished section of his notes, to peruse.

Reading through his notes, and especially where the Commander and the Governor were so effusively thanked, I paused. I had somehow hoped that my help might, in some small way, also be acknowledged, but I found that my name was not mentioned. I have to say that I was deeply disappointed. I blame myself for this, and also for the fact that there was a certain scornful severity in my voice, I am afraid, as I responded to the description of 'general excitement' on the part of the entire population of Chora'. To tell the truth, those few townsfolk who had come to have a look had soon departed, disappointed at the sight of mere earth and stones. I pointed this out to him, and I think he could hardly believe his ears at my presumption.

Yet I was as convinced as he, that this was indeed the famous tunnel which, together, he and I had discovered for the first time, after two and a half thousand years. Like him, I thought it extraordinary, astonishing, a wonderful adventure. The townspeople had come expecting something more visible, a great treasure perhaps, and had gone away disappointed. Well, they had not understood that the treasure was in the discovery. Others would understand, when they read of it, and it seemed to me that I could at least have been mentioned as having assisted.

Victor Guérin was hurt, and clearly did not at all understand my coolness. He returned to the work determined, he said, to uncover some more convincing evidence as he admitted, at least, that he could not make sense of the discrepancy in size of the 'tunnel' we had found. Maybe, I thought to myself somewhat drily, he simply had not yet understood the engineer's solutions to the geological problems of the 6th century BC.

*

Summer was coming to an end, with autumn gales beginning to set in. The weather changed, and it began to rain, heavily. Guérin went out to the excavations every day, knowing that he only had the use of the convicts for a limited time, but I am afraid I no longer accompanied him. The weather was too uncomfortable, and the area of excavation was a sea of mud.

It was clear, when he returned to the residence at the end of each day, muddy, wet and short tempered, that things were not progressing well. For myself, I concentrated on drawing, from memory, the scene of our first find near the chapel and the spring at Ayanni. I did hope that our history lessons might soon be resumed, but my tutor was not in the mood.

Two more weeks passed before the weather improved, and we met again in the evening, in the shade of the olive tree. Guérin had an announcement to make, but he was clearly nervous, although I did not know why. Nevertheless, he read out to me the continuation of what he had written and I listened in anticipation, hopeful of something more encouraging:

'*Upon resuming our investigations we had great luck, as, beyond a higher hill and then another ravine, we discovered a shaft dug down into the rock. It seemed to the Commander and myself that as it was situated on the same line as the canal,* it must have been dug originally in order to let light and air penetrate into the tunnel below. We hoped that if we could empty it of all the stones which had since piled up inside it, we could find our tunnel again.

Two of the convicts climbed down and worked for four days, digging out the shaft and emptying the stones and earth into a basket which two other convicts raised by means of a pulley and tackle. Once the shaft was cleared, it was found that it communicated with a horizontal vault, along which Commander Alexis and I were able to creep for about 29 paces.

The convict labourers tried their best to clear the tunnel in a southerly direction, that is, towards the ancient city. However, we soon perceived that the solid rock had ceased and we were once more confronted with an insurmountable obstacle of fallen rock and stones.

Two new openings were attempted higher up, which occupied the convicts for another week. The first of these gave no result but, at the base of the second, the carved vault in the rock reappeared. Unfortunately it was completely filled with earth and sand. The width of the vault was still the same: 80 centimetres. One of the convicts managed to worm his way along it, with great difficulty, for about 120 paces, literally dragging himself along the ground, but it was impossible to continue.

We searched for some time, hoping to find another shaft which would take us further into the mountain, but unfortunately we found none. I have calculated that it would take at least another month to clear even this distance and, alas, so much time is not available to us.'

Then Monsieur Guérin drew a deep breath. Avoiding my eye, he continued: *"It seems, therefore, as though we must now terminate our investigations."*

My tutor and I looked at each other in silence when he finished reading. It was now I, myself who stared in astonishment. I could not believe what I had just heard; I could not comprehend such faint-heartedness as this.

"But your investigation is a success" I cried out at him then, "you have said so yourself, and written it in your notes. We have found a part, at least, of the tunnel of Eupalinos of Megara, as Herodotus wrote. We have proved that what he wrote was true. How can you stop now? There must be a reason why this tunnel is so small, why it does not compare with the dimensions Herodotus gives. You must find out the reason. You must write it down for your public!"

Victor Guérin drew himself up. Of course he was not used to being shouted at, and I suppose he had quite misunderstood the intensity of passion which I felt for what I had all along thought of as 'our' project. He had looked for soft words from me, I know, but had twice now, been met with what, for him, Heaven forbid, almost sounded like criticism.

It seems he could not tolerate the thought that I did not seem to respect the professionalism of his approach. Very well, but I, for my part, found that I could no longer tolerate being treated as an ignoramus.

In truth, I am sure he was sick of the unlovely work on the tunnel which had begun to seem interminable in the mud and dirt. He longed for the beautiful columns and sculptures which he thought might still be found at Hera's temple, if he could only gain access to them.

Sure enough, he replied stiffly: "*Mademoiselle*, it may be that there is more important work for me yet to do on this island, and my time here is limited. I have urgent work waiting for me in Paris, of course, and there is much still to be done at the temple site, for instance."

I was in despair, and I turned away to try and hide my feelings. Of course his time was limited, I knew that. But could he not understand how I felt? I had been caught up in the romance of discovery and the life-giving delight of new knowledge, and had allowed myself to "open like a flower starved of light". I had hoped for more than this.

There was a silence, and then Monsieur gave a little cough of embarrassment. I searched for something more reasonable to say. In a way, I suppose we were similar, in that we both hated to be thought in any way disappointing.

In a softer tone he told me that he would try to do as I had suggested; perhaps he ought to write up a fuller explanation of the results of the investigation. All I could do was to nod mutely, and hold out my hand to shake. He took it carefully, intending to kiss it, I do believe, but I shook his firmly, and took mine away.

Upstairs, in my room, I rubbed my hand and stared out of the window at the setting sun, willing my anger to subside. I had been foolish and vain, I decided. It was up to me, now, so to mend matters that there could be no more possible misunderstanding between us. He was my teacher, I his pupil. No more, but also no less. I would ask him to reinstate our history lessons, to complete my education, as far as would be possible in the time left to him on the island. Then I would thank him, and he would go back to Paris, and my life would return to what it had always been. At the thought of this, the tears began to run down my cheeks.

*

The misunderstanding with his pupil had at least made Guérin aware that his report on the tunnel excavations might, indeed, be seen as somewhat sketchy. He thought again of how charmingly she had smiled at him, on that happy day at Aiyanni when they had first found evidence of Herodotus' 'copious spring'. Though still shocked at her presumption in criticising his work, he nevertheless decided to write up a fuller account of what had actually been achieved there, with a deeper analysis of the problem. He was a tender-hearted man and had allowed himself to construct a romantic fantasy which he could not now bear to give up. He thought, as he continued to write, that a rather more grandiloquent report would please Eleni, and he desperately wanted her to admire his work, as he thought she used to do.

'To sum up, then, although we had progressed about four hundred metres from the source, we only found a canal eighty centimetres wide, either cut into the living rock or, where there was no rock, walled and covered with horizontal blocks.

We would assume that, on reaching the mountain, it was no longer possible to sink shafts like the one we uncovered, the mountain being too high. So an access path would have been needed along its length, for the purpose of upkeep and repairs.

This would explain the tunnel width of 8 feet wide, as described by Herodotus. But what is the meaning of the 'second cutting thirty feet deep' which he goes on to describe? This is the problem which, so far, I am unable to understand.'

Poor Monsieur Guerin. He could not bear to imagine that he might have mistaken the small feed channel from the spring to the tunnel mouth, for the actual tunnel itself. Least of all could he bear to admit as much to Eleni. It cost Victor a great deal to admit to being so perplexed. Could she not understand?

'I believe it would take four or five months with ten or twelve workmen to discover the complete line of this tunnel, and a great deal more time and money to restore it, because of the numerous rock falls which have occurred over the centuries. This is the reason why, having very little time left, I have decided, with regret, to leave off these excavations at the tunnel.'

Would Eleni understand, and forgive? Tossing in his bed that night, Victor, normally so confident in his own decisions, was not sure.

*

XIII

Egypt or Sparta ?

THEODOROS HAS BEEN WORKING for some time on the carving of four magnificent fountains, confident in his friend's ability to succeed in finally getting the water from Ayanni to run downhill, through the finished tunnel, where it will be carried along a system of clay pipes which have been laid, till it reaches the city. These fountains have already been erected, in anticipation, at various points inside the city walls, where the townsfolk will be able to draw fresh water for themselves.

The day arrives when the Ayanni spring can at last be diverted into the channel so painstakingly prepared for it. All the labourers, the entire workforce, even the slaves, have come to watch at the spring-head over the mountain, where the water has been channelled into a reservoir. When the moment comes, Amoun is there, to direct the lifting of the large carved stone at the outflow. The workmen hold their breath as the ponderous stone is swung into place to block the natural stream; in theory, this should allow the water to flow directly into the channel cutting.

"Water will always find the way of least resistance." Amoun mutters the mantra to himself as he watches, his fists clenched.

As they watch, a trickle of water, growing quickly to a stream, gushes from the cistern at the spring mouth and down into the channel. The crowd shouts excitedly, as the water pours along the route made ready for it. Shouting and cheering, they follow its progress, at a run, around the ravine towards the mountain-side. There, it floods, at last, into the tunnel mouth, then disappears into the darkness.

The labourers clamber up the northern side of the mountain and race down the other side towards the city, to where Eupalinos is waiting with a crowd of citizens around him. A platform has been erected next to the innermost of the fountains, where Polycrates, accompanied by his bodyguards, has come to watch with Parthenope and the other palace women. The crowd is quiet as they wait, all eyes on the fountain.

They wait, and wait, but nothing at all happens. The citizens become restless, muttering, pushing. Polycrates' face is turning black as thunder, while Maeandrius the steward fusses and worries and tries to reassure the crowd. Eupalinos does not move, but stares straight ahead, waiting for Amoun.

Then gradually, faintly, from high up on the mountainside, there comes a muffled murmuring, almost a sigh. The people fall silent, straining their ears to listen, as the sound draws nearer and nearer, a rippling crescendo, the unmistakeable sound of running water through pipes.

Amoun waits for his master some way behind the press of townspeople who are jostling to reach the fountain and the water now pouring out, excitedly filling bowls and jars and water jugs. Eupalinos finds him, checks that all has gone well over the mountain, and the two of them make their way back along the main city street.

On either side, in the maze of smaller, cobbled streets and narrow alleyways of trodden earth, the sellers of wine and the cheaper prostitutes call out to passing customers. There will be plenty to celebrate today. Shrines to Hera, Samos' special protector, and to Poseidon, lord of the sea and of earthquakes, have been set up all along the main street, for thank offerings to be made.

Polycrates decrees a week of festivities for the whole town, and graciously commends Eupalinos for having made the city safe, no longer vulnerable in case of siege.

*

It is none too soon, for the political situation is growing more and more unstable. Polycrates knows that the system of checks and balances he has so painstakingly constructed over the years is fragile. Can he really rely on any of the complex alliances he has negotiated?

All eyes are on Egypt now, as mad Cambyses hurls his Persian hordes against that venerable kingdom. Fortunately for himself, perhaps, the Pharoah Amasis has died not long before the invasion, and has been succeeded by his son, Psamtik III. This unfortunate young man is taken prisoner by the Persian almost immediately. Besides the fearsome armies of his own empire, Cambyses has engaged a vast army of mercenaries: Greeks and Carians, Phoenicians and Cyprians, and has managed to arrange a treaty with the King of Arabia, who guarantees them safe conduct through the desert.

Inevitably, the Egyptians are defeated and Cambyses carves a swathe of cruelty through the country, forcing those who had opposed him to watch the execution of their sons and humiliation of their daughters, before they are themselves killed. Worse even than this, he violates the sacred places of the Egyptians, ordering Amasis' body to be taken from its tomb and subjected to every possible indignity. He orders

Apis, the sacred bull calf to be brought before him, then kills it with a blow of his dagger. Such desecration is unheard of: priests are whipped, ancient tombs broken open and sacred images burnt.

All the news is about Egypt and the horrors of Cambyses' mad, needless savagery. The people of Samos tremble in fear that he will turn upon them next, the richness and splendour of their court and the island's prosperity being too great a lure to ignore. But for once Polycrates has been looking in the wrong direction.

The attack, when it comes, comes not from the east but from the west, not from Persia but from Sparta and Corinth, who have chosen this moment to combine their strength and launch a powerful force, to land on the island and lay siege to the city of Samos. Never before, nor since, have the Spartans mounted a naval expedition so far from home, on this, the far eastern side of the Aegean sea, so close to Asia.

There will be much advantage to the attackers if their assault is successful: untold amounts of plunder to be had from the fabled riches of Polycrates and his pirate island, vengeance at last and restored pride after all the insults they have suffered over the years, as well as the suspicion that Polycrates might be making new overtures to the Persians. Above all, though, is the chance of annihilation of a rival to the coveted position of most powerful rulers in Greece. It is this political coup which Sparta has been so carefully plotting for so many years and now, with Polycrates distracted by the turmoil in Egypt, and with the help of Corinth and of those exiled Samians whom the Spartans have taken in, and who can now usefully be used as spies, it appears highly likely that they may succeed.

And somehow, this time Polycrates' spies have failed to warn him. He is unprepared and does not have time to get his ships under way before the Spartan fleet is sighted sailing swiftly along the southern coast towards the city. It is a huge fleet, and the Spartans, ready for war, are a fearsome sight. Stepping down from their ships onto the beach near the temple at Heraion, they make their sacrifice to the Gods, and prepare for battle.

In their shining armour, long hair and scarlet cloaks, the Spartans, acknowledged by all as the finest fighting force in all of Greece, are well aware of the morale-sapping effect they make. The Spartan force cuts its way through the small Samian shore defence with contemptuous ruthlessness and presses home its advantage, "*advancing forward to the gateway near the sea, on the side of the town where the suburbs are*", as Herodotus tells us.

Their phalanx is eight ranks deep and fills the entire area. The sight of such a vast number of fighters is truly terrifying. In tight formation the wall of bronze-clad killers advances along the Sacred Way, and the city defenders fall back appalled. Hastily they try to regroup, but by now they can neither advance nor retreat inside the city, as the gateway has been shut. The Spartan killing machine cuts them down like mown grass and their swords run with blood.

Wheeling round, yet still perfectly formed, the phalanx begins its advance up the hill towards the next point of entry to the city. A strong party of Samians, together with Polycrates' mercenaries, make a sally from the upper gateway on the ridge of the hill where, having the advantage of height, they manage to hold off the attack for a short time. But they cannot keep it up for long.

Disdaining the bow, which they consider a cowardly weapon, the Spartan infantry use their long thrusting spears in close formation to demoralize their enemies, following up with their short, leaf-shaped swords as they make their inexorable advance uphill, slashing, stabbing and killing the defenders as they come. The force of the Spartan attack is irresistible and the Samians fall back.

Even uphill, so great is the force of the Spartan charge, that, pressing forward after the retreating Samians, two of the leading warriors manage to hurl themselves past the gates and enter the town, before these gates, too, are slammed shut. Their own retreat now cut off, they are immediately set upon by soldiers and townspeople alike. Surrounded by the furious crowd, the two warriors place themselves back to back, fighting grimly, methodically, until the cobblestones run red with blood. They are cut to pieces at last.

Even though they are the enemy, however, such has been their bravery that the Samians, in admiration, will later honour these two Spartan soldiers with a public funeral, alongside their own fallen heroes.

*

All the gates to the city have now been barred against the Spartan attack, and the walls are impregnable. The Spartan and Corinthian troops parade for days outside the gates, showing off the perfection of their battle line and calling out insults and challenges, but they get no response. Eventually, they have no option but to settle down outside the town and prepare for a long siege.

How many days will the city be able to hold out? Not so long before, this would have been the Samians' greatest fear, but not any more. Water has now, for some time, been flowing into the town, through Eupalinos' tunnel, and the populace have enough and to spare, springing copiously from Theodoros' four fountains. And not only this, for such is the size of the tunnel (large enough for men and animals to pass through) that other provisions can also be brought in from the valley beyond the mountain, provided it is done in absolute secrecy and at the dead of night. And the secret is not told, no Samian spies will sell out to the Spartans; this ancient feud is too great, too deadly. Thanks to Eupalinos, Samos will not fall for lack of water.

The Spartan forces besiege the city for forty days. They continually challenge the tyrant to come out and fight, but for a long time they receive no answer. Polycrates has always preferred wheeling and dealing to open confrontation, and eventually decides to offer them money to go away. He has a large amount of money coined in lead, and has gilded it to look like gold coins. When shown to the Spartans, they judge it to be such an enormous fortune that honour will be assuaged. It is their custom to fight, not to sit around waiting, so, after much deliberation, they accept. (This, however, Herodotus tells us, can be nothing but a foolish story, as not even Spartans would be taken in by such a trick.)

When they see that the Spartan forces are leaving them, the Samian aristocrats who, this time, have taken up arms against Polycrates, lose all hope. In despair they, also, abandon the campaign.

Gathering all they can take with them, they sail away to Siphnos, then to Hydrea, and thence to Crete, always searching for a place to found a new city. Eventually they are attacked by the people of Aegina, beaten and reduced to slavery. The boars' heads on the prows of the Samian ships are sawn off and sent to the temple of Athena in Aegina. After this, there are no more reports of the Samian rebels.

*

Meanwhile, in Egypt, mad Cambyses has had an accident. He has been so long away from his kingdom that there has been a palace rebellion; two brothers, members of the ancient Iranian tribe of Medes, close kin of the Persians, have taken their seat upon the royal throne, and have given out orders to all troops throughout Persia and also in Egypt, that they should no longer take their orders from Cambyses. In a fury, Cambyses leaps upon his horse to return to Persia, but wounds himself in the thigh with his own sword while doing so. The Egyptian priests proclaim that the wound is in exactly the same spot where he had previously struck the sacred Egyptian bull-calf, Apis.

Be that as it may, Cambyses becomes convinced of his own imminent death and, indeed, gangrene eventually sets in to the wound, and he sickens and dies. The Egyptian campaign is called off, and the Persian troops return home.

Once again, then, it seems that Polycrates truly leads a charmed life. Will the Gods ever decide to punish him for his wickedness?

*

The celebrations and rejoicing after the Samians' triumph over the Spartans go on for a long time, uniting the people of the island as never before. Extravagant public funerals are held to honour the dead, attended by all the islanders, and the parties and debauchery at court grow wilder and more excessive.

Anacreon the poet composes songs and hymns praising the tyrant to the skies, and Polycrates is now more popular than ever. With his enemies departed, there is no more talk of rebellion; the tyrant's extravagance and despotism go unchallenged and corruption and depravity are again the order of the day.

In this time of general celebration there are many suitors for Polycrates' daughter Parthenope, who fall in love with her extraordinary beauty, but she is disdainful as ever, and will have none of them. Her father chides her for her sharp tongue and tells her that if she continues like this, she will never marry. Parthenope pouts, and turns away.

*

Eupalinos, expecting to be able to leave now that his work is done, finds himself inexplicably detained, unable to gain an audience with Polycrates to get the necessary permission to depart. It is a long time before Maeandrius the steward finally explains to him the reason for the delay.

The tyrant has understood that the tunnel is a fragile thing, subject to the whims and fancies of water spirits, and the tantrums of Poseidon Earth-Shaker. After such an investment in time and money, he is afraid to leave it unmaintained, and he expects Eupalinos, as the engineer in charge, to stay, indefinitely, to look after it. In this he is in fact not mistaken, as it has already become clear that lime sediment, deposited by the spring water, is beginning to build up inside the pipes, and the pipes themselves, having been laid in a great hurry at the last moment, may have some faults. There may be sections in the feed channel before the northern entrance to the tunnel proper, where they have been laid too close to the surface, and have broken or are in danger of breaking, letting in mud which is carried down the mountainside during heavy storms. The pipes must not be allowed to become clogged with mud and sediment.

Clearly, though, this is not the job of an engineer. Equally clearly, there is nothing Eupalinos can do to make the tyrant let him go.

XIV

RECONCILIATION AND RETRIBUTION

As the year descended into autumn and the days became cooler Monsieur Guerin and I managed to establish a kind of truce between us. The pleasanter weather helped; bright blue skies and cool, dry breezes drew us out of doors again and our disappointment gradually faded on both sides. A day came when Monsieur proposed that we take the donkey and climb up to the tower on the western ridge of the mountain, the only tower now remaining in the whole complex of towers and ramparts of the ancient city. As we set off I was determined to make this excursion a pleasant and good humoured occasion, making sure to keep the conversation animated but absolutely neutral.

Of all the other towers defending the city, only the foundations remained. Over the centuries, they had either been deliberately destroyed, had fallen as a result of earthquakes or had been robbed of their stones to build peasants' houses. Why had this one, single tower remained standing? This was a safe topic of conversation with which to animate our picnic as we sat on the side of the hill and looked out to sea, where rollers were breaking on the harbour wall, sending great plumes of white spray high into the air.

"Could this be a tower of the *'upper gateway on the ridge of the hill'* which Herodotus mentions" Guerin wondered, "when the Spartans attacked but were repulsed after a fierce battle?"

I agreed that this could be possible, although it seemed, to me, to be a very long way for heavily armed warriors to run up a hill, did it not? Guerin frowned, as I remembered too late that I had decided not to question anything he told me, any more.

There was no longer any sign of the 'gateway near the sea' further down, where the Spartan force first landed so I settled down to draw the tower, and the mountain behind it. I was trying to show in my drawing the solidity of the great square tower, visible from far out to sea, as would all the other towers have been, and the way it seemed to nestle into the ridge of the mountain, as though nothing could ever move it. "How much depredation must these mighty walls and towers have suffered over two thousand years to be so terribly destroyed," I marvelled "and at the same time, how extraordinarily well-built for even one of them to have survived!"

Monsieur was busy measuring the tower and recording it all in his notebook:

'To the west, about 100 metres below the summit of Mt Kastro, is a square tower. Although one or two of the top courses are missing, its present height is about 6m on the northern side of the mountain, and 8m on the south, as it has been built on a steep incline. A door leads into it, with a lintel made of one single block of stone, more than 2m long. There are 5 arrow slits in the walls, 2 facing west and 2 facing south, with one more to the north-west. The workmanship is superb: the marble blocks

of which it is constructed have been squared and finished with consummate art.'

"Of course, it *may* be", he mused as he wandered back to where I was sitting, "that this tower, so much better preserved than any of the others, is actually somewhat later in construction. It is quite possible, in fact, that the outside faces, at least, are in fact of Venetian workmanship."

I smiled and nodded in agreement, to show him that it did not matter in the least. There was still some of the sweet Samian wine left over from our picnic, which we finished leaning back against the walls of the great tower, resting a while before the long walk back to Chora. The breeze was cool on our cheeks, and the seagulls whirled and called as they dived above the breakers in the distance. Splashes of green grass were growing again where the rain had fallen over the previous weeks. It had been a pleasant day.

Perhaps it also occurred to Monsieur Victor Guérin, as we walked slowly back to where the donkey was tethered, that he, too, had been looking forward to this day. As he helped me up into the saddle he touched my hand, but I pretended not to notice. He led the way home in such obvious embarrassment, that I wondered what it was that I might have said this time, to offend him. However, by now I had decided that I would no longer allow myself to worry any more about such things.

*

We were seated again in the cool courtyard where we had first begun our history lessons. I wished to know what had happened to Eupalinos after the Spartans left. The ancient text which he had lent me was really too difficult for me to decipher, with its unfamiliar vocabulary and complex grammar forms, full of circumlocutions and digressions, so that to my chagrin I was finding myself more and more often obliged to ask my tutor for help.

I believe Monsieur Guérin had been happy to find that I wished our history lessons to be resumed. My constant interest and desire to know more must have been soothing to his self-esteem; he did not trouble to hide that for me to ask for his help was delightful to him.

"I have not found any further reference to Eupalinos himself" he replied, "but that he was successful in bringing water to the town we can have no doubt, since the Spartan siege was a failure. There are, however, several versions of the tyrant's eventual fate, of which the account in Herodotus is by no means the most frightful. Would you like to hear what I believe may be the most likely interpretation of what came to pass?"

I was all attention, and Monsieur smiled at me contentedly as he settled back in his chair, illustrating his lesson with expressive gestures as he warmed to the telling of the tale.

*

... ABOUT 522 BC

Oreotes, a Persian satrap, had been appointed Governor of Sardis in Ionia, on the mainland of Anatolia. It was the Great King Cyrus who had appointed him, which means that with Cyrus' son, Cambyses, dying and the succession to Persia's great throne in the balance, Oreotes is nervous now. With that dynasty at an end, whoever manages to secure the throne in the east, be he Mede or Persian, will be likely to redistribute the governorships of lucrative cities such as Sardis to his own men. Oreotes would like to find some notable cause he could take up which would demonstrate his loyalty to the Persian empire.

He is also nervous about the rise and rise of Polycrates, tyrant of Samos. For years, he has watched the little pirate island grow in prosperity and power, dominating the sea, holding magnificent court, attracting the flower of artists, sculptors, poets, and architects, its finger always on the pulse of politics in the Aegean. Samos is only just across the sea from the Anatolian mainland.

Oreotes suspects (and he is right) that Polycrates has plans to eventually make himself master of Ionia and the islands and he comes to the conclusion that Polycrates is a dangerous neighbour, not only to himself and the other Ionian satraps, but also to whoever becomes the next king of Persia. Samos would therefore be a safe target for him, but he knows he must proceed very carefully. He sends a messenger to Samos.

Polycrates is at table, feasting with Anacreon, when the messenger arrives. The man is a Persian whom the tyrant feels it is beneath his dignity to listen to these days, so he turns his back on him and continues eating and drinking.

"Once again golden-haired Eros strikes me with a purple ball, and calls me out to play" sings Anacreon, giggling. Perhaps Polycrates has drunk too much, or perhaps he feels the need to impress his lover, or is he perhaps just getting tired? Whatever the reason, dismissing the messenger is a bad miscalculation, as the insult now gives Oreotes a pretext for what he does next.

The second messenger is a Lydian named Myrsus, whom Oreotes feels sure Polycrates will receive. Though not a Persian, he is in the pay of the Persians, and hopes for a good reward for what he is about to do. On entering the palace, he catches sight of beautiful Parthenope and is instantly smitten.

Approaching her, he tries to attract her attention but she looks him up and down, then turns away laughing scornfully with her maids, and bids him not to come near her.

Myrsus is furious. Glaring at her back as she moves on proudly through the hall, he vows he will have his revenge.

As soon as he can, Mersus delivers a letter from Oreotes, as false as it is clever, appealing as it does to Polycrates' vanity, his hunger for power, and his greed for wealth:

'I understand, Polycrates, that you have an important enterprise in mind, but your resources are not equal to it. I have a proposal to make which, if you will adopt it, will ensure your success – and my own safety, for it is clear from reports I have received that the Persians are plotting my death. Come then, and get me out of the country; I promise you a share in everything I possess, and that will give you money enough to get control over the whole of Greece. If you have any doubts about my wealth, send whoever it is you most trust, and I will show him what I have'.

Polycrates cannot resist this. He sends Maeandrius the Steward to Sardis, with instructions to make a review of Oreotes' treasure. Perhaps the Steward, a solid but rather dull man, is not the best person to have sent, for Oreotes has filled eight chests with stones, and topped them up with a thin layer of gold. Maeandrius is impressed, and reports back to the tyrant that Oreotes is a wealthy man indeed.

How could Polycrates, himself so expert at exactly this kind of skullduggery, be fooled by such a trick? Yet he is fooled, or at any rate considers the risk worth taking, as he now prepares to visit Oreotes in person, leaving Maeandrius in charge of affairs in Samos.

His friends, advisors, courtiers and a horde of professional soothsayers all try to dissuade him from going. Parthenope, especially, claims she has had the same dream her father has so often dreamed: that he will be washed by Zeus and anointed by the Sun God Helios, and this dream has frightened her so much that she beseeches him not to go. She follows him down to his ship, screaming at him and prophesying dreadful disaster if he sets foot in Ionia. But he is adamant, sure of his own invincibility, and leaves.

The Gods observe, and decide that the time, at last, has come. They have been planning this punishment for a very long time, and they must make sure that it is sufficiently dreadful to match all the cruelty, corruption and injustice for which the tyrant has been responsible.

Somehow, Oreotes manages to separate Polycrates from his bodyguard. He is surrounded and caught, beaten, wounded, thrown down and trampled underfoot as he fights back to the bitter end. And his end is very bitter indeed. They kill him, at last, in the most agonizing and frightful way: he is impaled on a sharpened pole, then hung, still alive, from a tree and left to die, slowly.

He is a big, strong man and he takes a long time to die. As he hangs there, under the cruel sun, the moisture sweats out of his body so that he is indeed 'anointed by Helios' and later, as rain falls, he is 'washed by Zeus', just as the prophesying dream foretold.

*

In Samos, supreme power is now in the hands of Maeandrius the former steward, who has no idea what to do with it. If ever a man has so utterly misjudged a situation, it must be Maeandrius. When the news arrives of Polycrates' dreadful end, his cronies grab what money they can, and hurry away from the island. It is a cash drain on a huge scale.

Anacreon leaves at once for Teos, taking his favourite boys with him. Artists and praise-singers and mercenary armies leave to look for more profitable work, while men grown rich in the tyrant's favour pack up all their goods and money, so that soon there is not a ship to be had for the hiring, in the rush to get out before the crash. It is an economic and political disaster.

Maeandrius calls a meeting to remind the citizens that he is now their absolute ruler, but he is jeered at. Cat-calls and rotten eggs force him to retreat to the safety of the palace, and he begins to realise that he is in considerable danger himself. Deciding that he has no option but to retire from public life, he makes a further announcement that he has decided to become a priest. He plans to build a shrine to Zeus the Liberator, designed to show the people that they are free, at last, from tyranny.

But now Maeandrius' two brothers intervene, and persuade him to change his mind and hold on to what he has got. Thinking he ought to make a show of force, Maeandrius sends for all the remaining leading men of Samos, on the pretext of showing them his accounts, but when they arrive he has them all arrested and clapped in irons. He is torn between trying to appear strong, and fear of what may happen if he does. Finally, the strain of it all becomes too much: he shuts himself up in the citadel, and gives out the news that he is ill. His brothers, hoping to seize power for themselves, and taking advantage of his absence, simply have all the aristocratic prisoners put to death.

*

Back in Persia, there is a strong ruler on the throne again. Darius is the new Great King, and will bring order once more to much of the chaos left behind by his predecessor.

Syloson, Polycrates' younger brother, has been living in exile for all these years, ever since the tyrant had killed their elder brother and grabbed sole power. Now that both his brothers are dead, he thinks he can see at last the chance to regain the power which he feels is his birthright; he asks for an audience with the new King. Syloson and Darius had known each other when they were both young men, so an audience is granted. Syloson reminds Darius of a gift he once made him of a flame-coloured cloak. Would the Great King help him to recover Samos, his native land, which is now in the hands of a mere servant?

Under Darius, the Persians are once more turning their attention to the west, and in later years would even penetrate as far as Athens itself, but for the moment, the King is satisfied with the idea of installing Syloson as his puppet in Samos. Meanwhile, he allows a force to be dispatched to the troublesome island. To the soldiers surprise, they are welcomed in by Maeandrius, who has decided to ask for a truce by which he will be allowed to leave (with some pecuniary compensation), ceding the island to Darius to do with as he pleases. Accordingly, a number of high ranking Persians are sent; they arrive, and take their seats on the chairs of state.

And then Maeandrius makes another U-turn. He has changed his mind and allowed his brothers to persuade him that he should resist the Persian take-over. When the Persians take their revenge, as they surely will, he reasons, this will leave the island in a state of the greatest possible confusion for when it is handed over to Syloson, and this idea pleases him.

And so he and his brothers have the Persian ambassadors murdered. Predictably, the punishment for this is very terrible indeed. The Persian force returns, with orders to massacre every boy and man they can catch. And, accordingly, this is done. In one of his most memorable phrases, Herodotus tells us: *"As for Samos, the Persians took the entire population like fish in a drag-net, and presented Syloson with an empty island".*

*

I was appalled, but enthralled with the story. Monsieur and I climbed the mountain one more time, and sat again at a spot where we could look over towards the Turkish coast. The autumn winds were whipping the surface of the sea into white horses, and the sky threatened more rain.

Monsieur Guérin was once more in expansive mood. "It is interesting to note" he began, pleased as always to be able to demonstrate his extensive knowledge, "that Samos was always considered, in ancient times, to have been one of the most fertile islands. Homer called it 'watery Samos', while ancient writers have variously described it as *'anthemis'*, because of its flowers, or *'phylis'* for its greenery. It was also, of course, thickly forested with *'pityoussa'* and *'dryoussa'* which are pines and oaks, although these forests have almost all disappeared now."

I drew my shawl around my shoulders and wondered again at the misfortunes suffered ever since then by the people of this island.

"How has it come about," I demanded again of my tutor, but more gently this time, "that the island of Samos, more than any other Greek island, it seems, has suffered throughout history from invasion, occupation and expropriation?" And this time my tutor was only too pleased to expound:

129

Never again, he declaimed, since the reign of Polycrates, had Eleni's homeland known prosperity, but had been hounded down through the ages by a succession of oppressive regimes. They were conquered by the Romans, so that Samos, Rhodes and the islands between became a Roman province with a Roman governor, obliged to pay heavy dues to Rome in return for the 'Pax Romana'. Later, under the Byzantine empire, forbidden to keep a defence force of their own, they were constantly harassed by pirate raids from Saracens, Goths, Huns and Alans, and fell into deep poverty.

The crusades of the Middle Ages brought the island no relief: instead, they were a constant battleground for larger empires: invaded by the Venetians, re-taken by the Byzantines and then occupied by the Genoese. They were conquered by the Ottoman Turks, whereupon Samos was abandoned, as the inhabitants fled.

The island lay waste for a hundred years, but was then re-settled by the Turks, and Samians gradually returned. Yet under Turkish rule they were again attacked by the Venetians, and overrun by the Russians during the Russo-Turkish war. When at last, after four hundred years of Ottoman rule, the Greek war of Independence broke out, the Samians fought to the end, but were not granted their independence when it was given to the rest of Greece.

As we talked, of course, Samos was still under Turkish rule even though the rest of Greece had been liberated many years previously.

"What a punishment," I could not help exclaiming, "if that is what it is, for the arrogance and *hubris* of having aspired, at one time, to be the masters of the sea!"

On the way back to the Governor's house, we talked of the recent difficulties arising from insurgencies against the Turkish occupation, difficulties which had kept the Governor in Constantinople for much of the summer, and Victor took the opportunity to reminded me delicately that these difficulties, if they recurred, must inevitably hasten his departure from the island. I gave him no hint that this might in any way cause me distress, however, but I may have been unusually silent as we made our way home.

In fact I was not thinking of my tutor at all. My thoughts were still full of the story as he had told it. It had far too many unexplained non-sequiturs, I felt. What then had happened to all the other characters in the story and, above all, what had happened to Eupalinos? I went up to my room and took out my books, determined to see what else I could find. It seemed to me that I remembered reading a passage somewhere, which suggested other possibilities.

*

After much struggling with the ancient text, I thought I had found what I was looking for. The next day, immediately after breakfast, I brought the book to my tutor, and asked him to look over it with me.

"As for Maeandrius, he was sure of getting away safely any time he wished, by means of a secret tunnel, leading from the central fortifications of the city to the sea… thus it came about that he escaped from Samos on shipboard".

This was the passage which I had found in Herodotus' Histories, and I was anxious to know whether I had understood it correctly.

"*Mon Dieu*", was Victor's immediate response, "not another tunnel!" As always, he found me alarming when I became passionate, and felt offended that I should take it upon myself to put forward an academic opinion. He assured me that there had never been any indication of the existence of another tunnel and especially not on the seaward side.

"No, no" I cried, "not leading to the sea to the south, but from the centre of the city, heading northwards – what I mean is, not another tunnel, but the same one! If they were to go through it from the southern end, wherever that may be, but we know that it was inside the central fortifications, then they would emerge on the other side of the mountain, near to Ayanni. From there, heading eastwards, it is not too long a walk to the sea at Cape Katsouni, or even over to Vathy, where they could get a ship."

"And who might 'they' be?" he enquired, somewhat sarcastically.

"Well, Maeandrius must have taken Eupalinos, of course, and Eupalinos must have survived because otherwise how could Herodotus have known his name, and even his father's name?"

I sat down firmly on the window seat, looking triumphant. But Victor merely sniffed at the idea of such a contrived happy ending, as though History were to be treated as some sort of cheap romance!

And yet? What if my leap of imagination was in fact not so far from the truth? One could perhaps imagine an ending to this story which, while not actually spelled out by the ancient writers, nevertheless in no way contradicts their accounts?

*

Eupalinos and Amoun are down at the harbour, having been trying for days to get passage in a ship sailing for Megara. The quay is packed with people trying to hire ships, and the prices have gone sky high. There is confusion, and crowding, pushing and shouting, and Amoun, unable to stand it, keeps disappearing so that Eupalinos is constantly obliged to interrupt his negotiations to go looking for him. They are both exhausted. Night falls after another unsuccessful day, and they retire to where they have camped under a tree to share a loaf of bread together, as in the chaos, food too has become scarce.

They do not know what to do, for nobody knows exactly what is happening. Everyone had seen the Persian force arrive, and then leave again after their ambassadors had been installed in power. But the rumour this evening is that these ambassadors have all been assassinated, and that Maeandrius will take power again. Eupalinos finds this hard to believe. Surely the steward cannot be so foolish as to suppose that the Persians would ever let him get away with it? If the rumour is true, then it would be wiser to try to hide away than to hang about at the harbour, where they would be among the first to face the wrath of the returning Persian soldiers.

He sees a tall, lonely figure in the jostling crowd, and elbows his way through to find him. It is Theodoros, who has been looking for them. He himself has managed to buy a seat on a ship sailing for Ephesus in a few hours, and he is concerned at leaving his friends behind. There are no more places to be had on his ship, but he leans down and speaks softly in Eupalinos' ear.

"Find Maeandrius", he whispers, "he has locked himself inside the citadel, but the guards will let you in if you give my name. He always thought well of you, and you can be sure he has some plan of escape, should it become necessary."

They embrace and bid each other goodbye, as Theodoros prepares to leave. He will head for Ephesus, where he will take upon himself the construction of a temple dedicated to Artemis, almost as large as the Heraion at Samos. Towards the end of his life he will also design and help build the great temple to Apollo at Miletus, and will thus have been responsible for the three greatest temples of the Archaic period.

Looked at on a modern map, it is possible to imagine that these three splendid and beautiful buildings appear as the corners of a perfect triangle, covering the coast of Anatolia and the easternmost islands of the Aegean, and linking them together. Eupalinos must have smiled in satisfaction at his friend's achievement, if he ever knew of it.

Packing their few things together, Eupalinos and Amoun leave the crowded harbour and head for the citadel above the city. They find Maeandrius in a state of extreme nervousness, as news has just come in that the Persian army is massed in readiness on the shore of the mainland, and will set out for Samos at dawn. He appears unable to make any decisions, but they manage to persuade him that he cannot stay in Samos. Amoun is desperate to take refuge in the darkness of the tunnel, and this has given Eupalinos an idea for escape. Maeandrius insists on bringing with him his slave, to carry an impressively large amount of baggage.

Hurrying through the empty palace rooms in the abandoned citadel, they see a figure standing there, by herself in the throne room. It is Parthenope, proudly dressed in her finest robes, abandoned by her maids, who have all fled.

Amoun gasps at the sight of her standing there, so alone and so beautiful. He approaches gently, longing to be able to help her, but she turns on him, spitting contempt. How dare a servant approach her. She is a Princess, she tells him sharply, the Persians will respect her station. She will wait for them here, the invaders will take her to King Darius who will treat her with honour.

Amoun is distraught. He turns to the others for help, but Eupalinos takes him by the shoulder and urges him to hurry: they must leave now, immediately, or they will not be able to leave at all. Parthenope turns away from them coldly; she will stay where she is.

Night is falling. Quickly crossing the city, they reach the tunnel mouth, whose guards have abandoned it. They make the heavy door fast behind them, so that they will not be followed, and hurriedly walk the mile up through the tunnel which the engineer and his boy have walked so many times before, emerging at the northern end just as the moon rises. They stumble over rocks and through trees in the grey moonlight for what seems like forever. But Amoun knows every path and contour here, and he guides them towards the seashore on the east of the island. He whispers to his friends, the dryads of the trees, for guidance as they pick their way across stones and through dense forest cover and there is a murmuring in the branches, in response, though no doubt this is just the wind.

At daybreak, they hear the sound of screams and shouting in the distance, and they know that the soldiers must have landed, and are massacring and pillaging without mercy. Later, there is the smell of smoke and flames, and they realise that the citadel is on fire.

There will be little left of the fine city of Samos by the end of that day.

When they reach the coast they find themselves looking down at a few wooden huts at the end of a long beach, where a small stream trickles from the under the rocks and spreads out into the sea. An old man and a woman are standing uncertainly by the water, waiting as a good-sized fishing vessel pulls in to a ramshackle jetty. The old people's two sons jump down from the boat in alarm, preparing to defend their parents against the newcomers, if necessary, but Eupalinos talks to them softly, explaining what they need, while Maeandrius offers them a handful of gold coins.

Eupalinos, Amoun, Maeandrius and the slave crouch hidden in the bottom of the boat, in a puddle of sea water and fish guts, as they sail towards the northern tip of Samos. There the sailors swing the boat towards the west, for they are heading that way, out of trouble, and will take the fugitives as far as Delos. The sea turns dark but relatively calm and there are no stars that night. They try to sleep where they can, to the creak of ropes and the quiet slap, slap of the waves.

By now they hardly care which direction they take, as long as it is as far as possible from Samos, and the Persians.

*

It seems the Gods have taken pity on them and there are no storms on this part of their journey. Amoun is broody and spends the days on board gazing at the empty expanse of sea and trailing his hand longingly in the waves. After many days they reach Delos, where Eupalinos and Amoun will wait for a ship to Megara.

This is where they hear the news of the fall of Samos. It is a horrific story, worse than anything that could have been imagined, for the island, as writes Herodotus, is now empty. The Persians revenge is total: every single man and boy still on Samos, and every child, has been massacred while the women have been taken back to King Darius in Ionia. There they are being sold into slavery or shared out as concubines.

Amoun wonders about beautiful, unkind Parthenope. Will Darius have treated her with honour, as she seemed so sure he would? Or (as he dreads is more likely) is she now the concubine of some minor official such as Myrsus, taking both his pleasure and his revenge, as now he can?

*

Maeandrius will leave Eupalinos and Amoun here. He announces his intention of travelling on to Sparta. Why Sparta? It seems that he has had the extraordinary idea that the Spartans would be pleased to see him, as Samos can now no longer be a threat to anyone. He even hopes they might be persuaded to aid him in regaining control of Samos. He travels on and, on arrival, asks to see Cleomenes, the King of Sparta's son.

Cleomenes graciously accepts an invitation to the house where Meandrius is staying, where he is astonished to see a great pile of gold and silver cups and bowls, set out on the table. This, of course, is the loot which Meandrius gathered up in a hurry before leaving the citadel at Samos, brought with him by his slave. He begs his guest to take away as much as he pleases.

Cleomenes is no fool. Who in his right mind would side with Maeandrius? Disgusted at having been thought to be susceptible to bribery by a servant, he orders Maeandrius to leave Sparta at once and, in fact, to leave the Peloponnese. So, he is exiled and appears no more in any of the ancient texts.

*

While in Delos, Eupalinos offers up thanks to Apollo for their escape from the Persians and pays for an offering to be made at the God's high altar. He remembers also to kneel to Poseidon, begging for a good ship and a fair wind for the remainder of their journey. Will this be sufficient to ensure their safe return? On leaving, he feels unsure. He knows he has offended the gods more than once by his presumptuous tunnelling. Returning to the shrine, he makes a promise to Poseidon that if their ship arrives safely back in Megara, he will offer up a precious gift, in thanks.

They find passage on a cargo ship, carrying Naxian wine to Megara. At first, the going is good, with bright sunshine and a sparkling sea. As before, all those years ago on the outward journey, the ship stops off at Siros and Kithnos. Now it is late in the season and the Meltemi wind blows strongly, so that the ship fairly races along with the wind in the stern quarter, and the helmsman lashes the rudder to the rudder post to hold it secure.

But little by little, the sea roughens as the wind strengthens and shifts slightly, and waves roll in from the north-east, building up into immense troughs and crests, until at times the ship almost leans right over in its struggle to maintain an even keel.

The sailors call their passengers to move to starboard, so as to act as a counterbalance. Eupalinos is alarmed to see that Amoun seems not to have heard the order, but is standing up in the prow, his hair streaming in the wind, his arms outstretched to the elements, the rushing wind and the sea-spray. He calls him but Amoun does not hear.

Then a great wave, higher than all the others, hits the ship with a crash. Later, the sailors will tell how the wave resembled a towering running horse, its eyes ablaze, nostrils flaring, its mane a stream of white and silver foam. Sea water pours over the decks, then flows out through the gun-whales as the ship rights itself and continues on its course westward. The wind subsides, but Amoun is no longer standing at the prow.

Eupalinos hurls himself across the ship and stares frantically down into the depths, but there is nothing. Gazing out over the open sea, he can see a pod of silver dolphins leap and tumble in the far distance, and it seems to him that he can just make out a small boy riding on the back of one of them. The boy laughs in delight, waving back at him, as he watches, helpless. The image becomes smaller and smaller, then disappears at last into a shimmering mist on the horizon. Amoun is gone.

*

Their ship still has to sail across the Gulf of Saronika before going on to Megara. The wind has totally died; the sailors pull forlornly on their oars but they make little headway. To Eupalinos this journey seems to have gone on beyond endurance. What cruel trick were the gods preparing for him now? Clutching his head in his hands, and weeping, he finds that he hardly cares. Why take Amoun away from him? The offering he had made back in Delos had been a fair one.

"*Fair, yes*" whisper the waves slapping on the oars. "*Fair enough for Lord Poseidon to have heard you. A precious gift has been made, and the gods have accepted it*".

*

From far out to sea, the coast of Megara is flat, its sandy beach backed by olive groves and the high mountain range beyond. The wind has picked up a little, enough to round the island of Salamis. The sailors lower the sail, get out the oars and manoeuvre the ship into the port of Nisaea. So many years have passed since Eupalinos left.

The city has grown so that he hardly recognises it and he, himself, is hardly recognisable. Will his father still be alive? It seems unlikely. He shivers as he makes his way down the central street of the small town. So this is to be his reward for all those long years away from home. Will he find himself utterly alone?

He sees a taverna he remembers, goes in, and looks around. A group of men are seated at a table, and look up as he enters. They stare at him, and whisper among themselves, then make their way across the room.

"Eupalinos, old friend," he hears as he is clapped on the shoulder by a man he hardly recognises, then his hand is gripped by another, and another. The news of Eupalinos' success has spread before him, and he finds, to his astonishment, that he is famous now.

*

Naustrophos, his father, is at the doorway of their house, old and bent and leaning on a stick, smiling in welcome at his son.

"Did you think I would not wait for you, my boy? See, I am here, and there is work for us to do."

And indeed, it seems as though Eupalinos will forever, now, retain the favour he has gained with the gods. Together, in the years that follow, the old man and his son become much sought after for the design and building of aqueducts in and around the ancient city of Megara, and good fortune follows them in all their work. For hundreds of years hence, history will record, his name will still be remembered as "*One who brings things to a successful conclusion*".

Never again will he travel over the sea at the orders of a foreign tyrant.

XV

MA CHERE ELENI

IT SEEMS THAT MONSIEUR Guerin had already remained on the island of Samos much longer than he had originally intended. But now the summer had ended, and he was expected back in Paris. I saw that he had written in his notebook that *"serious family concerns obliged me to leave Greece, and return to Paris, even though I had been unable to complete my archaeological work".*

On the day of his departure, I accompanied him in the pony carriage, down to the harbour where his ship was moored. Standing on the harbour quay, he reached out at last to take my hands in his.

"Ma chère" he began *"or may I say, ma cherie?"* He did not know how to continue, standing there foolishly, as I looked at him coolly, waiting to see what he would say. But I did not take my hands away.

At last he asked me, would I consider, might I agree, would it be possible that I might... follow him to Paris? He would arrange everything, of course, and endeavour to make me comfortable when I arrived, he would introduce me to his friends in Paris; he could not bear to think that we might never meet again.

For one long, delicious moment I thought about it. Paris, city of fashion and culture, the Bois de Boulogne, theatres and concerts! Perhaps I could get proper drawing lessons, I would like to learn to dance. The idea of books and soirées and clever conversation, as always, made my heart beat fast.

But how could a penniless Greek girl possibly manage there? I knew very little French, I would be utterly dependent. Thinking of what such dependency must imply, the impropriety of it appalled me. I looked carefully at Victor: the slight corpulence, the fussy little moustache. Could I learn to love him? He was a well-meaning man, not unkind, but inconsiderate. It was his air of pompous vanity which had always irritated me: this offer felt as though he were granting me a favour, and I would never be free of the debt.

I knew I could not do it. Shaking my head as gently as I could, I thanked him, quietly, for his teaching and for his kindness, and withdrew my hands.

*

Victor bowed low, then turned and went on board, the manservant following with his luggage. I could see that he was very moved by our parting, but at the same time, secretly, I believe he was a little relieved at my answer. I imagine he felt that he had done something very romantic and dashing, but in truth he had no idea how we would actually have managed.

I climbed up the hill behind the harbour, to watch his ship sail away. Foolish woman, I thought, concerts and dancing, indeed. I almost laughed at myself. I watched from the hill as the white sail in the distance grew gradually smaller and smaller, and thought I could make out a figure at the stern, who might, just possibly, have been waving? A tear trickled down my face. I had made up a package of my drawings of our excavations, and given them to him as a parting gift, but he had not even mentioned them. Returning to the house at Chora, I found them still on the table in the hallway. Impatiently, I picked them up, and threw them into the fireplace.

*

Not long after Victor Guérin's visit, I left the Governor's house. Grateful as I was for their hospitality, I found I could not bear to remain in that tedious place one moment longer so I begged a room for a little while at the house of a lady friend of mine, recently widowed. She lived on the edge of the little town of Tigani, not far from the ancient harbour. Dear Cara; I do not know what I would have done with myself if she had not taken me in.

Wandering alone in the woods and pine groves near there, I spent many hours trying to think about what had happened. Should I, perhaps, have accepted the offer of a life in Paris? This was the question which would not go away. Perhaps I should write to Victor, send a hurried letter after him, saying I had reconsidered? And if not, then, what was I to do now? I felt myself falling into a mood of depression, impatient with the emptiness of my present existence, and angry with myself for this foolish vacillation.

I could not stay for ever with Cara; I had only a very little store of money and when that was finished I must either return to the Governor's house to beg for my old position again, or else, I suppose, throw myself off the top of a cliff to drown.

Solitude is a kind of poison, I discovered. I needed company and, even more, I needed some serious occupation. I determined to take myself in hand and do something useful, but what ? At the same time, I found I could not stop thinking about our tunnel; it had such a hold on me.

And, while I was still dithering, there came a letter from Monsieur Victor Guerin.

"My dear Eleni", the letter began, "I am returned to Paris, and am glad to say that the weather is very fine. I have been everywhere congratulated upon my findings in Samos, as I am sure you will be pleased to hear."

Huh, I thought. *His* findings, indeed. After some polite enquiries after my health, and that of the Governor and his wife, he mentioned that he had unfortunately left his favourite walking stick at their residence, probably, he thought, in the hallway? He had written to the Governor but had had no reply and he wondered if perhaps I might use 'my charms' to organise the expedition of the said walking stick back to him, in Paris.

I could scarcely contain my anger. I was disgusted even by the sight of his elegant copper-plate hand-writing. My friend Cara could not stop laughing, and in the end I am glad to say that I laughed too, but I am afraid I threw the letter into the fire-place, and let it burn quite to ashes.

*

There was a monastery over the hill, which I sometimes passed when out walking. It is not far from the spring at Ayanni where Monsieur Guerin and I had first discovered the ancient feed channel which must surely lead, we had thought, to the northern tunnel entrance. It was a quiet place, and over the following weeks I took to climbing up there in the afternoons to spend time in the monastery garden, under the peaceful shade of the trees. Of course, as a woman, I could not enter the monastery itself, but the garden was open to visitors. There was also a small library of old books where I was allowed to sit down to read as the monks became used to my quiet presence, nodding kindly when I walked up each day.

A priest whose name was Kyrillos Moninas was also a regular visitor to the library there. He was an avid scholar and historian, keenly interested in the local history of his island, which he had made it his life's work to study. Falling into conversation in the garden, we were both quietly pleased to discover the other's interest, both equally pleased to learn whatever we could.

We became good friends, taking long walks together, as I told him, bit by bit, of the abortive attempt to discover the whereabouts of Eupalinos' tunnel. We must have looked an odd couple, he in his flat black hat and long gown, but I hoped that anyone seeing us would have supposed I was receiving spiritual advice. He chuckled when he heard my story of finding the channel from the spring at Ayanni, and its inconclusive ending. "Oh yes", he said softly, "Oh yes, of course. Shall we go, then, and see what we can do?"

We went together to the source of the spring, following the line of the feed channel which I had helped to mark out with Victor Guérin. I showed Kyrillos where we thought the channel stopped. We scrambled around for a while in the undergrowth, but found nothing more.

"And yet", said Kyrillos, wonderingly, "According to my reading of Herodotos, if this is, as I suppose, merely a feed channel, the entrance to the main tunnel must surely be very near."

The next time I walked up to the monastery, I went directly to the library. I knew Kyrillos would be there.

"Do you know if there has ever been anything written down by local people, in years gone by, about our elusive tunnel?" I asked him, "any clue, however small, which might help me to locate it's whereabouts?" For such an idea had never occurred to Monsieur Guerin, so certain of his own abilities.

He replied enthusiastically: "If such a thing exists, then this surely would be the place to find it. The monks in charge of this library have always accepted anything to do with local history." He smiled at me kindly and added, "I will be happy to help you look."

The little library was cool inside, smelling of old leather and wax polish. Books were piled everywhere, even on the floor, so that it was difficult to find the space we required to search effectively. We looked and read, and tried to be systematic in our search, but we found nothing. In truth, we had no idea what to look for; there was simply too much to search through.

And yet I was enjoying myself immensely; I felt such pleasure in his company. Here is a real friend, I thought; this one does not try to show himself off, in fact he seems quite willing to follow my lead, if I wish. How delightful!

I suggested we return to the sunny little garden. What a pleasure it was, to sit quietly under a tree, with such a kindly person.

"It might be better simply to talk to the old people in the town," he suggested. "There may not be many great writers among them but they have very long memories, and they love to talk." So we made an appointment to meet together down at the harbour the following day.

Kyrillos was well-known there. It was part of his duties to interact with local people, to further the philanthropic work of the church. He was often to be seen amongst the fishermen and their families, talking to them or sometimes even working together with them as they mended their nets, drawn up in their brightly-painted boats inside the harbour wall. That day, waves were hurling themselves fiercely against the wall on the southern side, raising great plumes of spray high into the air and dropping back with a crash into the rough sea behind.

The contrast with the calm waters inside the harbour mole was astonishing. I remembered Monsieur Guerin telling me that this was thanks to Polycrates' poor prisoners of war, and I shivered.

After a while Kyrillos came back to the booth where I was waiting for him, accompanied by an old man whom he had persuaded to leave his work for a while, in return for a glass of ouzo. He was very old, and very dirty, and said his name was Dinos. He told us at once that he knew nothing about a tunnel, and held up his glass for another ouzo. Kyrillos nodded, called for a second glass and smiled at me to be patient.

"No, no tunnel," the man repeated, "but I do know about the pointed stones."

We shook our heads in puzzlement. What could he mean? He held up his hands in an upside-down V shape, and smiled triumphantly. We waited.

"The stones," he said impatiently, "The ones in the hillside, up past the meeting place and along a bit. My grandma used to say that you could get in behind there, where they used to go hide themselves, whenever pirates came, or thieving Turks." We waited some more but, seeing that no more ouzo would be forthcoming, he heaved himself upright, and shuffled away, back to his work.

Kyrillos took me by the arm and led me back through the little town. I asked what the man could have meant.

"I think the 'meeting place' that he mentioned must be the place where people sometimes used to gather, when there was any sort of public announcement to be made. It is hardly ever used these days, but it is still there, a long way further along this path. I can show you tomorrow. Some people say it was the Romans who built it, but I don't know; there are stone seats arranged in a large semi-circle, and a sort of platform in front."

I wanted to go there directly, but Kyrillos wished to check something first, he said. He needed to go back to the library.

*

By this time my friend Cara and I, sitting together in her comfortable little house, had told each other everything about ourselves. She was an excellent listener, and had already managed to make me laugh about my adventures with Victor Guerin.

"Should we also be laughing about your new friend Kyrillos?" she asked me wickedly. No, no, no, I told her; nothing like that at all, he was an excellent and extremely knowledgeable companion, that was all.

She put her head on one side and continued to tease me, until I became cross, at which she laughed all the more and said I was protesting far too much to be believed. I told her, then, how I wished I could find some profitable work to do. I wished I could pay her some rent, she could not allow me to be a burden.

She became serious at that. I knew that after her husband had died she had set up a little shop in the town, selling curios to the tourists who came every summer. They liked to buy printed postal cards, embroidery or pretty shells, sponges or any old thing which the fishermen dredged up from beneath the sea: pieces of broken marble, sometimes an amphora or two, pulled up from the sea-floor years ago. Her shop did quite well with the summer tourists, she said, well enough to see her through the winter, at least. She had seen some of my drawings, and liked them very much.

"Do you have any by you, at the moment?" she asked.

Of course I ran upstairs at once to fetch the cardboard case which held all my old flower drawings, and spread them out before her. In no time at all it was decided that I would mount them carefully and then I would come every day during the season, to help her sell them.

I was so excited at this prospect, that it was some time before I thought again of the road past the meeting place, and the 'pointed stones' in the hill.

*

When I next saw Kyrillos, he was outside our little shop, staring curiously in at the window. I ran out to greet him.

" So this is where you have been," he laughed. "I did wonder.

I was proud to show him my flower drawings, now mounted and displayed, by which I hoped he was impressed. Unfortunately, I had to confess that the 'archaeological' ones, pertaining to our discovery of the approach to the tunnel, had all perished in the fireplace at the Governor's house, in my fury at Guerin's premature departure.

He waved away my apologies. "Come," he said, "we need to find these 'pointed stones', and the space behind them, which the old fisherman told us about. There is still a track as far as the meeting place, and I have hired a cart to take us there. We will continue on foot after that, and search as we go if, indeed these stones exist".

I excused myself to Cara, who smiled mysteriously and wished us a pleasant journey.

The cart was standing in the shade above the harbour, not far from Cara's curio shop. As we left the town, I realised that we were following a rough track which lead west-wards, continuing on the southern, seaward side of Mount Kastro, quite on the other side from Aiyanni, where Victor Guerin and I had explored.

We passed through groves of ancient olive trees at first, and valleys full of sunlight and bright red oleander blossoms. The cart jolted slowly along and small lizards flicked and darted over heaps of warm stones beside us. I allowed myself to be calmed by the lovely, herbal perfumes of thyme and oregano crushed under the horse's hooves, and nearly slept, lulled by the rhythm of the rolling wheels. I awoke suddenly, as we entered a patch of shady pine trees, aromatic and spicy. There was the so-called meeting place, a jumble of broken stones in a sad state of disrepair. It was difficult to imagine it as a Roman amphitheatre. The carter stopped to let us down, and promised to wait until we returned. He could look forward to a pleasant afternoon's sleep while he waited.

The forest changed, darkening, as we walked on for what seemed a long way through the rough, thorny *phrygana* bushes, picking our way through the trees and undergrowth. There was no path. The shrilling of cicadas, pulsating in waves of sound, nearly deafened us as we stumbled on, for it was difficult going. I was wearing my stout walking boots but was not otherwise suitably dressed for scrambling among tangled roots and prickles and Kyrillos' black gown, too, was forever becoming caught in the bushes. The further we ventured, the denser the forest became until it was impossible to go further, but we saw no sign of any stones, pointed or otherwise. I asked Kyrillos again what old Dinos could have meant.

"I checked in the library," he answered wistfully, "and I thought we would find what we are looking for. There was a certain way of building in stone, with a pointed arch, described as typically 'Archaic' in style, and this Archaic Period fell between the eighth and the fifth centuries BC, that is to say, it spanned the period when Polycrates was tyrant of Samos. Yet where are old Dinos' stones, for I can see nothing like that here ?"

I could tell that my friend was as disappointed as I was. Every time we thought we were getting closer to finding our tunnel, it seemed to disappear again. When at last we returned to the 'amphitheatre', our carter was awake, and curious to know what had taken us so long. What had we been searching for, he asked?

I was feeling extremely tired by then, and cross. I replied glumly, "pointed stones", and I raised my hands together in the up-turned V shape which Dinos had shown us.

"Ah", said the carter, "you mean the place where the peasants used to hide, in the old days, when the pirates came? I will take you there now, if you wish."

Our faces must have been a picture, for the man laughed and shook his head in unbelief at our ignorance. "All the old people know of this place. They make sure we grandsons and great-grandsons remember the bad times! Who knows, they say, when it might be necessary again to hide from our enemies? Come, climb up."

We took a different path this time, somewhat lower down the hillside than the one we had tried before. I could feel Kyrillos's excitement, his tenseness and keen anticipation as we swung along in the cart, and somehow the forest did not seem so dark any more. Almost deafened, again, by the shrilling cicadas, we turned and laughed at each other, our hands over our ears. I was so glad to have my friend's company at this moment. Our carter was very merry, constantly warning us to beware of wicked pirates who might jump out at us from behind every tree, and chuckling to himself.

It was a long and tortuous way into the forest, before he pulled up the horse, and pointed, and at first I could not make out anything at all, other than thick undergrowth and trees. But then I cried out in excitement. In the distance, almost entirely covered over with thorny bushes and shrubs and deep in the shade of several huge trees, there was a large, shallow dip in the ground, behind a mound of tumbled earth and stones. Standing up in the cart, we could just make out the very top of a pointed stone arch, almost hidden in the dip in the side of the hill at the base of Mount Kastro. A rubble of rough stones, both large and small, was scattered around and in front of it. I doubt if we would have even seen it if we had passed by without knowing; certainly we could not climb up to it yet. Clearly, many years had passed since it had been used as a hide-out, as there was no clear path up there any more. It would need more strong hands than ours to clear all that undergrowth away, but never mind. We would come back.

"But what about the tunnel?" I blurted out. Is this the opening of a tunnel?" The carter looked puzzled. He shook his head. "I have never heard tell of any tunnel. My grandfather said there was a space behind those stones where people could squeeze behind to hide, even to stay a few days and nights, if they had brought provisions, but no, behind that, there is nothing but mud and earth and rocks, right up to the top. That's what he said."

*

Back in the town, it was a busy time at Cara's shop. There were plenty of tourists, and my flower drawings sold well. I was encouraged to go out and sketch some of the town's older buildings, even to add some colour: warm sepia for the stones, and intense blue for our beautiful Greek sky. These were very popular, and I was able, triumphantly, to pay Cara some rent at last.

She enquired several times how my 'tunnel hunt' was progressing, but I believe she really wanted to know about another kind of progress: that of the relationship between myself and a certain friend of mine. I had no intention of telling her anything at all.

Of course, however, it was always on my mind. As that summer drew to a close and we were no longer quite so busy in the shop, I walked up to the monastery again, and enquired after Kyrillos. He was away on church business, it appeared, some sort of diocesan gathering on Patmos, or one of the other islands, and would not return for a while, no one seemed quite sure as to exactly when.

I was forced to go home and resign myself to waiting for him. I was astonished to find myself so very cast-down. How presumptuous of me to assume that he would be immediately available, merely because I wished it to be so.

Cara had fixed up a little bell on the door of her shop, which tinkled whenever a customer came in, but it was some time before it tinkled for me. I spent those intervening weeks drawing and colouring happily, and getting used to 'keeping shop' for Cara, but I longed for some sign from Kyrillos, to show that he had not forgotten our quest nor indeed, hopefully, my own anxious self. Perhaps he had grown tired of my demanding, importunate ways. I had not forgotten how cross Victor Guerin would become, whenever I dared to raise my voice.

He did come, at last. I had not even heard the bell tinkle, but I looked up from my work one day, and found him there in front of me, with his warm smile and his lovely, kind brown eyes.

"So here we are" he said, very gently. I was so pleased to see him; I just smiled back.

*

Kyrillos had not forgotten about our quest, far from it. He had brought me a map of the island of Samos, with an enlarged section of the south-eastern part. He spread it out on the table and explained to me his idea.

"Look, Eleni," he said, "Here is the track where the theatre, the old meeting place is, remember?" I nodded.

"I have made a rough estimate of the distance that the carter drove us from there, west-wards beneath Mount Kastro. See? I have marked it with a cross about where we first saw the pointed stones. If, as may be the case in spite of what our carter told us, and the pointed stones do mark the southern end of a tunnel, then it must surely run northwards from there." I nodded again.

"I now draw a line towards the north, right over the mountain, in the direction of Aiyanni, where you showed me the spring." He took my pencil from the desk, and drew his line.

"It seems to me that we must find the other end of the tunnel somewhere along that line, must we not? At a point, surely, where our line and your feed channel will cross."

It seemed almost too simple, but I could find no fault with this idea, especially as it meant that I would be obliged to take the rest of the day off work in the shop in order to go back over the mountain with Kyrillos and down the other side to Aiyanni, a lovely walk of several hours in which to enjoy his company.

*

Cara was annoying me. I loved her dearly but I was becoming impatient with her constant winks and smiles whenever I mentioned our tunnel, or indeed anything related to that topic, such as my own enthusiasm and determination to finish what I felt I had begun, or even just the pleasure I took in walking over Mount Kastro on a fine spring day. As for any talk concerning the subject of priests, or the priesthood, she would tease me unmercifully. At first I simply refused to entertain that subject with her at all, but this brought me no relief, only increased irritation. I would have to have a straightforward talk with her, I realised. So, I told her.

Kyrillos had been married some years ago, but he was a widower. His wife had died, of a cancer, I believe. I am not sure of the details, and would never wish to pry. In our Greek Orthodox Church, a priest may only ever marry once. Celibacy is the norm, but married men may be ordained to the priesthood. However, married priests who lose their wives after their ordination are not allowed to re-marry. For a man like Kyrillos, honest and devout as he was, it had been clear to me for some time that there was absolutely no way around this.

I do not mean by this that Kyrillos had ever brought up the subject with me nor, certainly, I with him. Nevertheless we both knew by then that our friendship was very special, so special indeed that I could not bear to have it winked at and joked about any more. This I explained carefully to Cara.

He was just the most agreeable person I had ever met. I loved to spend time with him, he was so unassuming and yet so quick and clever, and I knew he enjoyed my company as well. Why otherwise should he be willing to spend so much of his time with me, searching for something which may actually never even have existed, for all I knew, or at any rate, might have been utterly destroyed centuries ago? When he smiled at me, his eyes crinkled up at the corners; he was always good-humoured. We were able to laugh and joke together; in short, I loved his company and we were the best of friends. This would be enough for me.

Cara wrinkled up her nose at me and patted my hand. But, indeed, I meant what I said.

As for finding the north end of the tunnel, it had seemed such a good idea. We tried, many times, climbing in a more or less straight line over the mountain top and down the northern side, but it was not easy; there was always so much undergrowth and tangle of trees in our way. We did not, of course, have the means to clear the area or to excavate; we just relied on Kyrillos's extensive knowledge of the area, and whatever I could remember of my studies with Victor Guerin. Kyrillos' work as a local historian was taken seriously by the Monastery librarian, and was even recognised as far as Athens. He had written a number of pamphlets and articles, and it gradually became accepted that I was his assistant, unorthodox as this may have seemed.

Chatting pleasantly together, as always, we searched for years for another hidden opening, trying to locate that northern entrance, but as time passed, our quest became less and less urgent. Several times we came upon what looked like an opening in the north side of the mountain, completely overgrown and blocked with fallen earth and rubble, but we never could find the real thing. And yet, in the end, it did not matter much. We each came to value the other's companionship more and more, and eventually our search for the northern entrance became just another pleasant exercise, to be indulged in whatever free time we were able to take together when the weather was fine.

I have never regretted those years; for me, they were perfect. Kyrillos and I remained for ever the very best of friends, although I doubt if Cara ever believed me.

*

THIRTY YEARS LATER

(1884)

AND SO THE ENTRANCES to the tunnel remained as they had been for centuries: hidden behind rocks and undergrowth, entirely unexplored. In my day, they were still completely hidden behind the impenetrable *skania* trees and bushes, and this was how we had left them. And yet, this is not quite the end of my story as, thirty years after Victor Guérin's visit, another archaeologist came to Samos to explore its ancient monuments. This one was a German academic from Athens, Ernst Fabricius.

I suppose that he did not read French, as he does not seem to have known anything about Victor Guérin's work. He enquired from the local people as to the possible whereabouts of the tunnel of which Herodotus wrote, and was advised to ask at the monastery, where he was introduced to Kyrillos. Thirty years is a long time, and my friend had now grown old.

"My dear Sir," he replied to the German gentleman's questions, "I would be delighted to help you, if my legs were still strong enough. However, I would suggest instead that you contact Miss Eleni; she is the one you need to talk to."

Dear Kyrillos, still so generous, as always. I am no longer quite so young myself, but of course I was delighted to take young Fabricius to see the spring at Ayanni, which was still bubbling up from the ground and trickling merrily away along its channel. Then I showed him the place where Victor Guerin had marked out the feed channel. He made extensive notes of all this.

"I am sorry I cannot show you the tunnel entrance itself," I explained, "It must be somewhere near this end, but we have never found it."

The young man thanked me for my help and bowed, formally, promising to send me a copy of his notes when he had written them up.

I have heard since, that the north entrance was eventually found, rather further into the mountain than where we had searched. I was surprised to learn, too, that the stone arches at the top were not pointed, like the southern ones, but rounded. Why was that? I asked Kyrillos.

"Ah, now that is interesting," he said. "Rounded arches are a Roman design, so this must mean that our tunnel was still in use centuries later, after the Romans had taken over all this part of the world. Maybe the northern section fell into disrepair, and they would have had to repair it, in their own fashion I suppose. Fancy! Eupalinos would have been surprised, would he not?"

Not, perhaps, I thought, as surprised as he would have been if he could have known of our own explorations, another thousand years later!

With the help of Kyrillos's map, young Fabricius was also able to make his way to where we had told him of the 'pointed stones', on the southern side, and he came back to show us his own map, with the two entrances linked by a straight line over the mountain. Such a very straight line! I thought to myself, then, that surely no one could be certain of the *exact* shape or direction of the tunnel underneath that great mountain, dug out so very many centuries ago, with such primitive means, and in such difficult terrain? But I had long ago decided that this was now no longer my problem; no doubt future generations will make up their own minds about it.

Kyrillos and I walked out to the monastery garden and sat as usual under our shady tree. The sun was warm, but not too hot, a lark sang high up in the sky and the breeze made ripples in the long grass. I tucked a blanket around my dear good friend, looking forward to another long, delightful afternoon sitting together in the soft sunshine.

"Thank you, *agapi mou*, my dearest," he smiled, "I think we need not worry any more about our old tunnel now, do we?"

I smiled to myself then. I would not appear in any of Mr Fabricius' notes, I knew, just as I had not appeared in any of Victor Guerin's notes, but what did it matter now? For the rest of my life, I will be able to carry with me the comfortable conviction that, without my help, the mysteries of this extraordinary tunnel might never, truly, have been uncovered.

And if Victor Guerin had not introduced me to the riddle of the tunnel and then gone back to Paris, I would never have left the Governor's house, and if I had not left, I would never have become acquainted with Kyrillos, and if I had never met him, I would never have known the happiness we have together. At this thought, I nearly laughed out loud: it seems that after all, I have to thank you, Monsieur Victor !

How Cara will laugh when I tell her this.

*

159

EPILOGUE

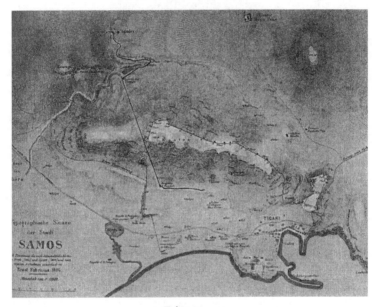

Fabricius map

FABRICIUS' NOTES AND SUBSEQUENT findings, together with a clear map of the area showing the location of both the north and the south entrances to the tunnel, were published in 1884. The presumed route of the tunnel itself, however, as Eleni noted, is marked as a straight, unbroken line.

For as we have seen, neither Guérin, nor Fabricius, nor Eleni herself had understood the real marvel of Eupalinos' mile-long tunnel: the fact that it was actually built as two tunnels, starting from opposite ends and meeting in the middle. In fact, quite possibly even Herodotus knew nothing about that, either, nevertheless reporting it as *"one of the greatest building and engineering feats in the Greek world"*. This it most certainly was, as it seems to have lasted for at least a thousand years, before first falling into disrepair.

We know from the archaeological evidence that it was used for a time by the Romans to carry water to the town and, later, as a hideout from attack by marauding pirates, but after this, it seems, the tunnel gradually filled up with mud and the entrances became overgrown. Then another thousand years passed.

It had to wait until the 1850's for Monsieur Guérin to appear and note at least the existence of the feed channel and, thirty years after that, for Ernst Fabricius to map the northern and southern ends of the tunnel, as well. Yet neither of these two had realised what a marvel of engineering they had actually found, both of them assuming that the tunnel was built just as one straight line without a break, from north to south.

In Eleni's day, the landscape of Samos looked very different from what it does today, being still entirely covered in thick forest as it had been for centuries, so it is not surprising that the two entrances proved so hard to find for our 19th century explorers. Then in the years 2000, 2007 and 2010 fierce forest fires devastated the southern side of the island, and the covering of trees is only now beginning to come back.

Meanwhile, modern entrances were constructed at both ends, for safety reasons, somewhat obscuring the ancient stones. To the north, a modern house has unfortunately been built over part of the spring at Aiyanni (Aiyades), and a chapel, dated 1879, now mostly covers the ancient cistern itself, but a small portion of the arched covering of the original 6th century BC feed channel can still just be seen, if you look hard for it.

It was not until the 1970's, with the excavations by the Deutsche Archaeologische Institut of Athens, that the entire length of the tunnel was carefully excavated and the middle section, where they meet, was fully understood and mapped. At last, the whole tunnel was cleared and opened to visitors.

But then, another serious rockfall occurred. Were the gods angry again? Was Poseidon Earthshaker jealous of this new interference with the tunnel through the mountain he had thought to reclaim?

For years, the tunnel itself has had to remain closed for reasons of safety; although visitors could enter from the southern end, it was only accessible for a relatively short distance, far short of the twisting middle section, which is the most interesting part to explore. Treasures such as the beautiful accuracy of the great carved stones which hold up the roof were no longer open to the public. Eupalinos' extraordinary calculations, marked in red paint on the walls, could not be seen.

Tourists were puzzled, and climbed back up the ancient stone steps at the southern entrance, worn down by the tread of countless feet during its thousand years of use. Emerging blinking into the bright sunlight, they turned to each other and wondered what was supposed to be so special about this dark, narrow hole in the side of a hill.

But then, in the summer of 2017, something hugely important happened. Funded by the EU's National Strategic Reference Framework program (NSRF), at a cost of over 3 million euros, this colossal, magnificent, splendid monument has once more been cleared, and opened to the public. Safe, but unobtrusive walkways have replaced the former ugly iron railings over the lower tunnel containing the clay water pipes, now clearly to be seen. Sensitive lighting illuminates the whole, beautiful length and especially the amazing central part where the north and south tunnels meet together. To enter it is an extraordinary and unique experience.

We must hope that the Gods, this time, will approve.

Sketch of Eupalinos' tunnel, showing the north and south entrances and the curved meeting point

AUTHOR'S NOTE

STARTING WITH HERODOTUS' STATEMENTS about Samos, quoted on the first page of this book, I have relied on his '*Histories*' to tell the story of Samos and its greatness in the 6th century BC. I have used the Penguin Classics translation by Aubrey de Selincourt, who states that "*Its main theme is the heroic struggle of a small and divided Greece against the mighty empire of Persia*".

The technical information on the actual construction of the tunnel comes from Professor H. Kienast's archaeological report: *The Aqueduct of Eupalinos on Samos*, published as a Guidebook by the Greek Ministry of Culture.

The information gleaned from Monsieur Victor Guerin's notebook is from my own translation of his book: "*Description des Isles de Patmos et de Samos*", published in 1855, two years after he left the island.

The character of Eleni is my own invention, as is that of Amoun, Eupalinos's apprentice. All the other people in the story are actual historical characters, appearing in one of the three main sources quoted above.

About the Author

Dr Jane Schofield studied archaeology at Oxford and at Gottingen University in Germany. She taught modern languages in France, Germany and England, before emigrating to Australia where she was a lecturer at the University of Newcastle, NSW.

Now retired, she and her husband Neville visit Greece and the islands of the Aegean every year.